THE FRENCH FIASCO

JUSTINE FRENCH MYSTERIES

MYRTLE MORSE

BRITISH AUTHOR

Please note, this book is written in British English and contains British spellings.

BOOKS IN THE SERIES

The French Fraud
The French Folly
The French Fiasco
The French Fancy

1

THE UNSURPRISING PARTY

It was a beautiful day in August when I received the strange invitation. Being a psychotherapist, the mysterious inner workings of the human mind were usually mysteries easily solved, but I'd needed to read this particular invite several times before I'd come close to understanding it.

Damien Rue, a fellow expat and an antique weapons enthusiast, had asked me to come to his birthday get-together on the 12th of the month. He'd also suggested that I might want to bring along a certain local chief of police, as the other guests would be interested to meet him and it would give the chap a chance to practise his English. I'd paused to laugh out loud at that comment - which would have Marius spitting feathers if he ever heard about it. I was pretty sure that English passing Marius' lips voluntarily was about as likely as France booting out its president and returning to a good old fashioned monarchy, because they missed the fancy crowns and gowns.

It was the next part of the invitation that had been harder to decipher. According to Damien, his party would most likely be held in the old barn behind his property - the one he'd never got round to renovating - and it might be a buffet or a barbecue, or something along those lines. It would be an intimate event with other local British expats, because his birthday was one of their biannual meet-ups. He wasn't sure about what time it would begin, but I should try to get there for eleven o'clock in the morning, and if I was early, we could have a drink together. He wished he could be more specific, but the party was a surprise.

"Damien Rue has invited me to his own surprise birthday party," I'd said out loud to my dog, Spice, who'd cocked his head in that charming way dogs do to show they're paying attention.

The more I'd thought about it, the more I'd realised it was in keeping with Damien's eccentric character to invite me to a party he wasn't supposed to know about. While I'd been flattered that he considered me a close enough friend to ask me to come, I'd been a lot less sure about the idea of a day spent with a group of other Brits. I had nothing against my fellow countrymen and women, but there was something that made me grit my teeth about people who'd moved to a foreign country and insisted on sticking exclusively to those with whom they shared a common language - and very often not a whole lot else.

Damien must have guessed my misgivings, because he'd added that he was planning to make a sumptuous mid-morning tea with homemade cakes and biscuits that he'd be delighted to share with me. I'd smiled and shaken my head, knowing that my new friend had definitely got my measure, if he was using the promise of food as a bribe to get me to come to his party. I'd called Damien and told him I would love to attend, but I'd also done the courteous thing and kept Marius out of it - knowing he would likely be treated as the party's entertainment and a quaint local curiosity.

I'd kept him out of it... until he'd threatened me with a

fine for not banishing the last remaining splatters of exploded manure from the front of my house. He'd claimed this fine was because I was 'bringing down the local area' - which was pretty rich considering he'd said it with his back turned to the many and varied rusted carcasses of farm machinery, which littered the wasteland outside the house opposite mine.

The threat had arisen because I'd been needling him to do something about a local moonshine maker. I'd experienced a sudden influx of therapy clients - all of whom reported seeing monsters while they went about their daily business. I'd quickly worked out the common denominator and found the name of the perpetrator, but Marius had been less than keen to take them down… mostly because the guilty party was his uncle. That was the problem with being the one and only police agent in the same small town where you'd grown up; when it came to laying down the law with your family, you risked Christmas Dinner becoming a rather awkward affair. Whilst I'd initially empathised with his conundrum, his response had annoyed me into asking him to come with me to Damien's surprise party. He'd reacted predictably (with unconcealed horror) and that had been the end of that.

Or so I'd imagined.

"I don't like it," Marius said, frowning and squinting at the grey rendered house with its bright red door.

"Really? I think Damien's kept the place looking wonderful. I wish my neighbourhood was this tidy, and the lavender bushes by the path are blooming so beautifully. Do you think there's a deeper reason why you don't like it?" I asked him and received a glare in response.

"I don't mean the stupid house! I mean this stupid party. And stop trying to get me to open up about stuff. I don't need therapy."

"You didn't have to say yes to the invitation. In fact, I was close to certain you would say no, which was the only reason I asked you to come," I confessed, better late than never.

"I'm obligated to be here to make sure Damien doesn't let anyone wander off with one of his weapons again. Or maybe he'll snap and go on a rampage" he added, brightening at the thought of being able to arrest a man, whom he'd long wanted to lock up over his laissez-faire attitude towards keeping his more dangerous possessions secure.

"Well, look who's decided to open up about his feelings!" I couldn't resist teasing. "I think you're really here because you want something to go wrong, so that you can complain about it, because you enjoy complaining," I informed him, exercising the right of friendship to tell Marius a hard truth about himself.

"First of all, everyone enjoys complaining - it should be classed as a hobby - and secondly, I'm a totally normal person and there's absolutely nothing wrong with me, so stop trying to stick me in a box," he complained - immediately proving my point. He gave his old enemy the lavender bush a kick when we passed it on the way to Damien's front door.

"I'm not sure that it is all that normal to actively enjoy complaining. Also, it would be abnormal for someone to be completely normal," I said, pretending to consider all of this seriously whilst Marius rolled his eyes. When you worked as a psychotherapist, it was good to have some people you could talk to who didn't take you seriously all the time.

I shook out my ashy curls and smiled down at the pink bow on top of the wicker basket I was planning to give to Damien. It was a basket that was not exactly small or light, and I was carrying it all on my own. Marius strolled along with his hands shoved into the pockets of his dark jeans - but who needed chivalry in this wondrous day and age of equality?

I decided to stop being peeved with Marius, remembering that today was supposed to be a celebration for a friend. Worrying that the chief of local police was going to try to sabotage it in some way would only result in me failing to enjoy myself - something which I knew would upset Damien the same way it would upset me, were our roles reversed. Social butterflies thrived off positive reactions but struggled when others around them failed to mirror their buoyant mood.

I let my worries go with a sigh, taking a moment to look around at the straw-coloured fields that surrounded the property. The summer had already been long and warm, and rain scarce enough that the yellow hue was evident in all areas where no watering cans or industrial sprinkling systems were present. Damien's house was in the middle of a huge expanse of land that was occasionally used for crop planting, but more often as pasture for Limousin cows - when it was used at all. Creuse was the kind of place where you could drive for ten minutes and not see anyone else on the roads - and even by local standards, Damien lived remotely. The only other car Marius and I had passed on our way here had been a silver Mercedes parked off to the side at the start of the very long, not exactly paved road that led to Damien's house and an assortment of farm buildings and barns in differing states of repair.

I pressed the doorbell, making sure I stepped well back from the door itself to avoid its unusual outward swing - courtesy of Damien modifying it to open outwards, so that the fancy rug he'd placed in the entrance hall didn't get scuffed. Whilst I waited for the birthday boy to put in an appearance, I wondered if I'd got his present right. Usually, I was pretty good at things like presents. It came with the territory of being a psychotherapist - being able to figure out what made a person tick meant you could also guess what they might want as a gift. When you paired that with my talent for observation and noticing when items were old and worn, or missing altogether when required, I privately (and not very humbly) considered myself as something of a gift queen. When it came to Damien, I was a lot less certain. Mostly because I'd found the perfect gift for him but had known better than to actually buy it.

Normally, I enjoyed duelling with Marius over our differences in opinion, but it would probably push him over the edge if I'd presented Damien with the rather lovely trio of ancient Bo-shuriken throwing knives that I'd seen on an auction site. Damien loved the stories behind the weapons he owned, and these three blades had a corker of a tale to go with them - involving assassins and spies, but I'd forced myself to take my finger off the 'bid now' button and reconsider.

With the spectre of Marius accusing me of encouraging Damien's eccentric hobby, I'd instead opted for food and drink, which was probably Damien's second greatest love. Being the daughter of a French chef, I was thrilled that Damien was a connoisseur of French products - unlike the kind of expat who'll pay a small fortune for a tin of beans to be shipped across the channel. Having said that, I did occasionally crave custard creams, so even I was not completely immune from missing what I'd left behind.

"Well, helloooo!" Damien said, flinging open the door in a manner that made me glad I'd taken precautions, revealing a dazzling red and gold dressing gown - that surely had to be one he reserved for special occasions. I silently stowed the inspiration for next year's birthday present in my brain. Damien wore dressing gowns no matter what time of day it might be.

I handed him the hamper basket with a smile and thanked him for inviting us. Marius grunted something and looked away when Damien gushed over how pleased and surprised he was to see the local chief of police.

"I don't mean this offensively... but I didn't think you'd really come. Socialising and parties aren't normally your scene, are they?" Damien said, marvelling at Marius, like he was a rare historical artefact dug up from Machu Picchu.

"This event needed police supervision," Marius replied, grumpy that he'd just been called antisocial - which he definitely was.

Damien glanced at me to see if he was joking, but I kept a straight face - only just managing not to roll my eyes. "You really didn't have to get me a present," Damien said, hastily clearing his throat when Marius continued to pout. He weighed the basket in his hand and looked delighted by the heft of it. "Just you coming here to socialise with me and a few friends is a gift, but thank you," he finished, making it very clear that he was certainly not refusing the present

"It's from both of us," I added, knowing that Marius probably couldn't wait to jump in and tell Damien that he certainly hadn't got him a present.

"No, I got you something of my own," the chief of police said, astonishing me by stepping forward and taking his hand out of his pocket. There was a misshapen metal blob sitting in his palm. We all stared at it in contemplative silence for several seconds. "It's a bullet," Marius explained when no one came up with the answer he evidently considered to be obvious.

"How thoughtful," Damien said, still sounding just as mystified as he would have done had Marius told him it was a pencil sharpener.

"It's already used, so you can't cause any trouble with it," the chief of police continued, not helping to sell his gift. "It's a bullet that was used by the Maquis du Limousin resistance fighters, during the Nazi occupation of France in World War II."

There was another silence, but this one was a lot more shocked... because Marius had actually brought Damien a wonderful, thoughtful, and rare gift.

A gift that I hadn't thought of.

"How on earth did you get it?!" Damien asked, his eyes filled with excitement as he delicately took the bullet and examined it.

"It's a great story involving a daring rescue I made. A farmer used to keep this bullet on a shelf above his outdoor toilet. One day, the wood above the cesspit had rotted enough that when he sat down, the entire shed just..."

"I think the story behind the bullet itself must be fascinating," I interrupted, deciding that Marius' interesting story should probably be kept free from further details.

The chief of police shrugged. "To cut a long story short, the farmer didn't want to go anywhere near that cesspit ever again, or touch anything that might have been pulled out by chance at the time of his rescue, so... I got to keep the bullet."

We all looked at the flattened piece of metal again... which was now in Damien's very clean hand.

"Well, thank you... I'll treasure it," he said in such a way that made me think it would be treasured *after* being dunked in bleach. "Come in, come in... you don't mind if I open this hamper now, do you? The others will probably be along soon enough, but I've never grown out of enjoying unwrapping things," our host said, diving into the basket and cooing over each and every item he pulled from the deep pink tissue paper I'd used.

"You have wonderful taste, Justine," he said, kissing me on both cheeks when he'd finished. "I will have to hide it from the vultures. I have plenty of other things for them," he said with a twinkle in his blue eyes. He swept an arm around the banqueting hall he'd built when converting the barn, highlighting the birthday cards that covered every surface and unwrapped gifts neatly piled up on the vast table at the centre of the room. The predominant theme of the cards seemed to be Union Jacks, shoehorned into the card design in every thinkable way, and the presents included Scottish shortbread, tea, and a tin of biscuits shaped like a London bus. There was even a small, old-fashioned pistol that had a cameo portrait of the Queen set into the handle.

Marius walked over to inspect the gun - probably to see if it could be confiscated - while Damien raised his grey eyebrows at me. "I don't know why they all think they need to send me reminders of dear old England. I haven't been back there in yonks!"

"They're probably projecting their own worries onto you. People imagine that there must be an awful lot that you miss and had to leave behind," I said, able to see why Damien's friends and family back in Britain might think that there could be no greater disaster than running out of tea branded with an image of the Yorkshire Dales.

"Oh, I know they all mean well," Damien gamely agreed. "In any case, I have French friends who are endlessly curious about products from the UK, so nothing will go to waste." He strolled over to the red bus biscuit tin and frowned. "Although, some things may be banished to the back of a cupboard."

"Did you see anyone else on your way here?" Damien called from the kitchen after he'd offered to make us some tea or coffee. Damien's coffee was always excellent, so I'd opted for the latter. It might also have been because I'd noticed Marius glaring at the Big Ben tea caddy someone else had bought Damien.

"There was a car parked by the entrance to your road, but it was very far from your property. An old, silver Mercedes

Benz," I added, able to visualise the scene perfectly in my mind.

"That sounds like Fern Higgle's car," Damien said slyly - apparently correct about his own surprise event. "She only came here four years ago, but since then, she's been the organiser of just about everything for our little expat group. My goodness! If she's parked that far away, she really is committed to the idea of the party being a surprise this year. I hope she managed to bring everything across the fields okay. I'll have to tell her she very nearly got me going. I almost believed that there wasn't going to be a surprise party at all! Still... we would have had a fine old time of it, just the three of us - especially when you brought such a splendid gift. Plenty to drink, and the only policeman for twenty miles around us is right here - so he can hardly arrest anyone for being a little over the limit, if he's joining in!"

"I'm going to pretend I didn't hear that," Marius replied, almost managing to break out of his huff. I hid a smile, knowing that Damien was deliberately speaking French for his benefit and was trying to pull the chief of police's leg.

"When are you going to find someone else to work with you, Marius? The word on the street is that you somehow convinced our Justine to help you tidy up the station, but isn't there anyone you can recruit to take your old role? Any poor sap at all?" Damien intoned from the relative safety of the kitchen.

Marius looked like he might be on the cusp of a small explosion when he heard the same question that he'd undoubtedly been hearing ever since he'd become the town joke - a chief of police without any police agents to order around.

Mercifully, Damien gave up this topic as a lost cause and the conversation turned to other local gossip that the host somehow always seemed to be kept abreast of, in spite of living out in the sticks. Time passed with coffee and cake and no further lighting of Marius' vast array of short fuses. I wanted to talk to him about his search for another police agent in more depth, but I worried he'd just accuse me of interfering, or trying to get inside his head. With each and every passing day, I feared Marius was beginning to resemble his bad tempered predecessor, and I knew that neither of us wanted that to be the case - not when Marius loved his hometown and had always dreamed of doing a better job than the last chief of police.

The knock on the door came a minute after we'd all heard tyres crunching on the loose stones outside of the house and car doors slamming. When the hollow thuds reverberated around the room, Damien shot us a wicked grin and practiced his best 'surprised' expression, which made me snort into my second cup of coffee.

I didn't know it then, but the real surprise was yet to come.

2

BEIGE BUFFET

"Surprise!" the group of people on the doorstep shouted in English when Damien opened it in his opulent dressing gown and threw his hands up in the air, acting the part of a totally shocked recipient of a surprise birthday celebration. Knowing Damien, he'd probably honed his skills for this very moment at the local amateur dramatic society.

The Brits poured in, humping a hamper between them, which they set down on the table with a flourish.

"We all clubbed together and got you a few bits we thought you'd like. Happy birthday, old chap!" a man with wispy brown hair and a thin moustache said, walking over and shaking Damien's whole arm. A gold tooth winked in a beam of sunlight when he smiled.

"We've arranged a surprise buffet in the barn across the field for you. It's probably going to be ready soon," a woman with dark blonde hair added, glancing at her smartphone and rolling her eyes when she saw that there was no signal. She dumped it back into her *Chanel* bag and pursed her subtly painted lips.

"My goodness! Where on earth did you find all of this?!" Damien exclaimed when he opened the most recently delivered hamper. I glanced over and inwardly raised an eyebrow at the proliferation of products that you would normally find in any given corner store in the UK.

"There's a depot in Guéret that sells all of it. None of it's cheap, but only the best for you, Damien," a man with hair that seemed impossibly dark said, flashing pearly white teeth. He was tanned for the region's temperamental weather, and the black stud earring in his left ear winked red for a moment when a beam of sunshine from a window caught it, perhaps hinting at a wilder youth.

"You shouldn't have," the birthday boy said graciously, before catching my eye. "Really, you shouldn't."

"No trouble at all," the guests gushed, while I had to fight to keep a straight face.

"I must introduce you all to Justine and Marius whilst we're waiting for this buffet to be ready. Are you sure we shouldn't go and help with anything?" Damien asked, looking around at the group, who turned to face a young man with premature streaks of grey in his brown hair that was already springing up from where he'd pressed it down with a comb.

He pushed his oblong glasses further up his nose, awkward under scrutiny. "Fern said she'd be fine doing it on her own when she left our apartment this morning. You know how she likes to do everything herself. It's the journalist in her - she doesn't want to share the credit with anyone else." When he didn't elaborate beyond that, all eyes returned to Damien.

"Righty ho then. Where were we? Introductions! This is my good friend Justine French, and her special friend Marius Bisset - who also happens to be Sellenoise's chief of police. Justine is a psychotherapist who has spent far too much time unravelling the knotty minds of our local community. Sellenoise will be the sanest town for miles around once she's finished!"

"You can come and sort out my hamlet when you're done with your town," the man with dark hair said. "They're all nutters. I can't even dig one little swimming pool without my neighbours running to tell tales to the local mayor. I would understand, but they've all got illegal swimming pools, too. There's probably someone I need to give a backhander to."

"Calm down, Henry, there's police here," the wispy moustached man told him with a chortle. "Those sideburns are a blast from the past. I can't believe Miranda allowed you to grow them!"

A woman with dark red extensions that curled at the ends, who'd been trying to decide whether to pull the front of her dress up or down, looked up at her name. "Don't look at me. I popped to Paris with some girlfriends, and they were there when I got back."

"Don't throw rocks when you're standing in a glasshouse, Derek," Henry retorted with a big smile on his face.

Derek's hand immediately shot to his small moustache. "Ursula likes it."

The woman with the *Chanel* bag shot the man, who must be her husband, a skeptical look. "I never said I liked it. I tolerate it. And you."

Unfortunately, I didn't think she was joking.

"I was hoping for the quiet life when I moved here, but the woman next door is forever poking her nose over the fence, trying to see what I'm up to. It's pretty hard for her to see anything because she's a good half a mile away, but... I know that's what she's doing," a woman with fly away mousey curls interjected, her eyes moving back and forth between the other speakers in such a way that made me think she was probably making it up in order to try to fit in.

"It's because nothing ever happens," Ursula agreed, pushing her blonde locks back over her shoulder. "We're like reality TV to the people around here."

"I'm Lyra, by the way," the woman with the wayward hair said, deciding to turn her attention to me and introduce herself - unlike the others. She twisted her bracelet made of buttons nervously and seemed only too aware of how out of place she looked standing next to someone like Ursula, or even the more gaudy Miranda.

"Alex," the man with brown and grey hair spoke up, placing a hand on his chest and nodding at me and Marius. "I'm normally here with my fiancée, but as you've probably heard, she's busy with sausage rolls and cold chicken nuggets."

Damien tried to conceal his horror over the forthcoming beige buffet. "Did you catch all of that?" he asked, wanting to check I'd be able to put names to faces.

"I think so," I told him with my best shot at an encouraging smile. This was Damien's party, and it would be important to him that everyone was having a nice time. I glanced over at Marius to see how much he was understanding of this conversation, but he was inspecting a packet of crumpets with a look of incredulity on his face.

"Well, how about we all have some tea while we wait for Fern to pop in? There are some lovely biscuits in the hamper you brought that I would be honoured to share with you," Damien said, managing to make it so that he got rid of his less than wanted gift in a subtle way. "We mustn't spoil our appetites, but I'm sure a few biscuits won't do us any harm. It's so nice to be back together again. How long has it been?"

"Christmas was the last time all of us were here, but the ladies do like their little gossip group," Derek said, trying to get some eye contact going with Henry.

I noticed Lyra look down at the floor when the 'gossip

group' was mentioned, making me think that she probably wasn't always included.

"Who are these people?" Marius said to me when he'd finished glaring at each and every single weapon hanging on the wall of Damien's great hall.

"Be nice," I said through gritted teeth, knowing that I would need to take my own advice today. So far, my not very open mind towards other expats had closed even further. There may be some hope in the form of Lyra and Alex, and seeing as Fern was the sort of person selfless enough to be organising an entire buffet by herself for Damien, I rather suspected that I'd like her, too.

"How's the toy business going, Derek?" Henry asked, pretending to be serious.

"They're sculptures, and very well, thank you. How's cleaning people's pools and fixing their broken windows going for you? Has anyone asked if you're the one breaking them in the first place?" he replied, needled by the other man's comments.

Henry laughed, apparently not as insecure as Derek. "Take it easy, big D. I'm just having a bit of fun."

Ursula sighed audibly and exchanged a look with Miranda, but when she spoke, it wasn't to her friend. "Lyra darling, how is your job treating you? Does it feel strange being at a party with someone you work with?" she added, glancing across at Alex and arching her neatly plucked eyebrows in a way I thought was probably intentionally suggestive.

"We work in different departments," Alex jumped in, shooting an apologetic look in Lyra's direction.

"Don't you think Fern has been rather a long time?" Damien asked, sensing that the conversation urgently needed a new direction.

Once again, everyone looked at Alex for the answer.

"Well, she said she'd come and get us when she was ready. I mean, she hasn't called or messaged to say there's an issue, but there's zero internet or phone signal here," Alex said with a shrug. Everyone else present rolled their eyes and muttered about the inconvenience of this particular issue, which they all claimed would never occur in the UK. I was starting to wonder if this bunch were not expats at all, but something closer to missionaries sent to France to wax lyrical about how good things were back in Blighty in the hopes of converting the locals.

"Maybe we should go and check on her?" I suggested - noting the general shuffling of feet that followed because no one much fancied accidentally being co-opted into helping set up.

"Excellent idea," Damien agreed, happy to have someone backing him up.

"Fern doesn't like it when people interfere with her projects," Alex said, suddenly looking strangely nervous about heading over to the barn uninvited.

"She'll be fine," Ursula said, giving her head a single shake and looking obviously annoyed by the man with oblong glasses. "You worry too much."

"You can't worry too much when there is always something to worry about and many excellent reasons to worry about it,"Alex muttered, but no one except me heard him. The others were already heading to the door, now that Ursula had made the decision for the group.

"We're going to the barn," I informed Marius - who was doing a great job of being completely zoned out. I did wonder why he'd come in the first place, if he didn't intend to try to join in, but I discovered I was grateful for his presence - one of only a few people present who didn't seem fixated on how France could be so much more than it was right now… so much more… *English*.

But then, hadn't I also accused Marius of enjoying complaining about everything? There was no news as good as bad news, as the press liked to say, and most people - including the guests at this party - enjoyed sharing their small miseries and disasters. Hearing about how wonderful someone else's life is seldom makes for gripping conversation. People generally prefer rehashing tales about the time when someone nicked their underwear from the washing line, or how their house is haunted by the ghost of Cleopatra - even though they live in Yorkshire.

The warmth of the day hit my skin when we crossed the wild flower field behind Damien's house that separated the property he'd converted from the one he claimed he wanted to renovate, but had never found the time. Even though Damien's own converted house was large enough for social gatherings and guests, I suspected he rather enjoyed having the option of an even more rustic social venue in the form of the old barn. Plus, it meant people could arrange 'surprise' parties for him.

I'd glanced over at an ancient tractor and trailer that was doing its utmost to return to the land, when a black and white cat darted in front of Marius, tripping him up. He landed on his face in a clump of crown daisies. "Do you own anything that's not a lethal weapon?!" he complained to Damien.

"Orwell knows a sucker when he sees one," I informed Marius with a smug smile.

"How about you tell us what it's like policing in your town? I used to work in security before I found my true calling, but that was in London, so we probably saw more action in a day than you do in a year. What's the latest big case? Killer cow on the loose?" Derek asked, laughing at his own bad joke, which I then felt obligated to translate for the mystified chief of police.

I slapped Marius' hands away from trying to grab whatever mayor-sanctioned weapon he'd decided to bring along as his plus one to Damien's party. That was the other problem with Marius being the only member of the one man local police force - there was no one to keep an eye on him. *No one... except for you*, I reminded myself.

"Urgh! This bag's full of food that should have been kept in a fridge," Miranda said when she glanced into a bag that had been left in the grass in front of Damien's barn. "The sun's got to it. There's melted butter everywhere."

"Fern probably forgot to bring it in because there were so many things to remember" Alex said, shaking his head. "I did offer to help, you know... a bit, but she insisted on doing it all herself."

"She always does," Ursula commented with a dramatic roll of her cold, grey eyes. "Fern doesn't think anyone can do anything as well as she can do it herself... even if it's their job that they've had years of experience in."

"She got the engagement ring she wanted, even if it wasn't entirely genuine," Alex said, looking sheepish when Ursula spoke up about a past event that he'd evidently endured.

"She's probably too stubborn to admit she hates it. No one wants to wear a fake ring, Alex. It tends to say a thing or two about the relationship it symbolises," the other woman preached back.

"That sounds like the sort of propaganda someone whose livelihood relies on them flogging shiny pieces of rock would be indoctrinated in."

"You have no taste," Ursula said, wiggling her fingers where three different rings twinkled in the sunlight - diamonds, sapphires, and little black stones all worked harmoniously into metal. Where is she?" she added, frowning at the tightly shut barn door and directing her annoyance towards it.

"Don't you remember from previous years? Fern always closes the barn doors and bars them behind her to stop Damien from peeking," Henry said, flashing the birthday boy a wink and taking a couple of steps forward. He shoved the doors, which shuddered but made no progress inwards. "See? She's in there. It just means she's not ready for us yet."

"If she's not ready, surely she'd have said something by now. We've hardly been quiet," Ursula countered with a frown on her face.

Something had started to ping in my brain after the discovery of the abandoned bag. From what Fern's friends had said about her, organisation was her forte, and the idea that she would have forgotten what was quite an essential detail to the buffet seemed... wrong.

"Fern?" Henry yelled, doing a very good job of making himself heard. There were probably sheep three miles away who'd just looked up from their grazing.

We all listened to the silence that followed.

...A silence that was punctuated by the sound of liquid steadily dripping onto the floor.

"Perhaps she's had an accident," Lyra said, her hands fluttering to her face. "We have to get inside!"

"It could just be part of the surprise," Miranda commented with a careless shrug. "Damien said it himself... he knows exactly what we get up to each and every year. Perhaps she's trying to scare us all."

"The doors are stuck?" Marius said to me, frowning as he failed to follow the conversation, but perceived the important part.

It was Damien who answered him. "We may be in a bit of a pickle. I do believe that with the assistance of a ladder from the house, we could climb up to a window. There's absolutely no point at all in trying to force…"

Marius charged towards the barn doors. The rest of the group instinctively moved out of his path, before he flung himself through the air. His shoulder hit the ancient wood of the barn door with a thunk… and bounced straight off, causing Marius to rebound like a very solid cabbage thrown at a wall.

Damien cleared his throat when the chief of police got up and tried to pull out whatever weapon he was carrying for the second time. "As I was about to say… there's no point trying to force the doors open. They were built to be barred from the inside, or latched from the outside - which I've always found curious. Perhaps during a time of war, the inside bar was considered a defensive safety measure for anyone seeking shelter. Or maybe the reason it can only be latched shut from the outside was to stop anyone from becoming trapped inside, should a bar ever accidentally slip down." He gestured to the flimsy looking latch on the exterior of the doors. "Perhaps we could push the doors inwards just enough to be able to slide something into the gap and have a go at lifting the wooden bar. It's hinged, sort of like this…" he explained, laying his arms one on top of the other and making the top one swing up and down.

"There's a metal rod in the trailer behind the abandoned tractor," I said, remembering the rusting pile of junk that I'd focused on for a second before Marius' tumble. There had been a stack of slim metal rods of unknown purpose all the way over to one side, quietly oxidising in a stubbornly remaining puddle.

"Right… my goodness! Let's have a go!" Damien said, looking completely thrilled about how his surprise party had genuinely taken a turn for the unexpected. Clearly, not everyone shared the sense of foreboding I felt.

That drip.

There was something bad about it.

Derek fetched a rod and brought it back, approaching the door confidently until Lyra surprised me by stepping forward and swiping it from his grip.

"What... does this require a degree, or something?!" Derek complained, but he stepped back while Lyra examined the rod. With practiced precision, she pressed inwards on the doors and slid the metal pole through, angling it and using the latch to help her get the leverage she needed.

"Something's blocking me... wait... got it," she said after several moments spent wriggling the rod around and levering it upwards.

We all heard something fall heavily to the ground on the other side of the double doors. Lyra frowned and tossed the rod away, giving the doors a solid shove and revealing what had made the noise when the bar had been lifted.

And what a reveal it was.

It was now that I realised why the dripping sound had made me so uneasy. Water drips in a light and fluid way, but something far more viscous makes a different sound as it collects on the bare earth floor of the barn in a large puddle. Blood sounds different. I focused on that pool of red, because I wasn't ready to look at the other thing that had fallen into view when Lyra had pushed open the doors.

There were gasps and moans from the rest of the onlookers. They froze with horror, no one moving to investigate further when it was obvious that help had come far too late.

"We should go inside and secure the scene," Marius said quietly into my ear. I managed to nod before carefully picking my way around the slowly spreading pool. Only a dip in the packed dirt floor had stopped it from flowing out beneath the doors - which would have been a decent clue that something had gone terribly wrong with the buffet.

When I walked into the barn, I couldn't help thinking that Fern had finally succeeded in surprising Damien and his guests.

All except for one of them… who'd known the punchline before it had been revealed.

3

A RIGGED GAME

Fern was dead.

Not just dead, but very dead.

I steeled myself as I looked at the horror scene in front of me, feeling as though I was observing my own reactions from somewhere beyond my body. I needed my brain to get over the shock and start working. I needed to think clearly, because this moment would never be repeated. Some evidence has a very short shelf life before vanishing forever. With Fern's fate exposed to the light of day for the first time, now was the best moment to solve what had happened to her.

Technically speaking, the 'what happened' part was exceedingly obvious. A medieval halberd tied to a cable had swung down from somewhere up above and hit her in the back - with enough power that Fern had previously been pinned to the thick wood of the barn door, like an unfortunate butterfly inside a collector's picture frame. It was the spear part of the halberd which was responsible for the impaling, the outer tip of the axe blade remained pressed, flush against her back, but not embedded. *The killer should have just used a spear,* my practical mind chimed in, apparently focused enough to run critiques of murder methods. A label attached to the shaft of the weapon had a familiar name written on it, but I'd been expecting to see it. After all… who else left halberds lying around?

When Lyra had struggled to lever up the bar, it had been because Fern had been pinned in an upright position by the weapon. Aided by Fern's weight and Lyra's levering, the pointy blade had been dislodged from the wood. Fern's corpse had fallen to the ground, before being unceremoniously clouted when the doors had been opened.

As far as crime scenes went, this one was already a mess in more ways than one.

"She would have been standing there to lower the bar across the door," Marius said, breaking the silence and indicating the fresh cut in the wood of the barn door, where Fern had hung, waiting for someone to find her.

I nodded in agreement, noting the way the bar swivelled on one end, so it could easily be lowered and raised - just as Damien had indicated. "Look! There's more than one impact," I observed, carefully skirting the blood and pointing to the splintered wood in two close, but distinctly different, places. "This murder was rehearsed."

"Oh dear, that's my halberd," Damien said, popping his head around the corner and spotting the oversized weapon that still protruded from Fern's back, even though she'd ended up lying on her side.

"I don't suppose you'd like to save us all a lot of hard work and effort by confessing to killing this woman?" Marius suggested.

"Do you think it could have… fallen from somewhere? I'm almost certain I left it propped up in a corner," Damien said, his eyes darting back and forth between us and his other guests, as he wondered if he was unknowingly directly responsible for the death of one of his friends.

"I don't believe that this was an accident," I told him, deciding that he didn't deserve to be left in suspense. My eyes scanned the interior, whilst Damien waffled about how terrible and unexpected this all was - all the while still describing it as a horrible accident, which was his mind trying to process the initial shock. Clearer thinking came later for most people in the event of sudden trauma, but I had made a career from noticing things, even in the worst situations. Like right now, I'd spotted various pulleys and attachments that someone had added to the beams that criss-crossed above our heads, forming what must have been an elaborate boobytrap with a trigger somehow attached to the action of a person lowering the bar to shut the door behind them. *That's something which every single guest knew was Fern's custom,* I thought, remembering that it had been mentioned and no one had expressed any surprise.

"I'll call the gendarmes," Marius said when he'd finished processing the scene in his brain. "Tell your British friends not to touch anything and keep them all out of the barn! Nothing should be touched!" he added in my direction, repeating his command for emphasis, no longer even half-heartedly attempting to cover his disdain for the expats. Unfortunately, I had to concede that his disdain was probably well placed in this instance. Even though this trap had been set up by someone in advance, which meant they hadn't needed to be present to commit the crime, the prior knowledge of Fern's annual routine implied that she had been killed by a person who'd known her well... someone, who was probably standing in the field outside of the barn right this second.

"How did everyone arrive at the party?" I asked when I walked out of the barn and found the group loitering in an awkward silence. Marius had told me to keep them away from the crime scene, but it didn't seem as though anyone else was keen to get a closer look - which was probably a wise choice.

"Alex got a lift with Derek and me, because Fern had taken the car. Miranda and Henry came together, and Lyra came alone," Ursula supplied. Her face was white, but her mouth had set in a line where she was keeping a tight leash on any emotions that might have been threatening to wriggle loose. "Alex said she was fine this morning," she added - as if that meant she couldn't possibly be dead now. She shook her head a second later, acknowledging the nonsensical nature of her own words. "Who could do something like this to someone else?"

The answer to that question would be the focus of an investigation that was about to begin. Someone had decided to murder Fern Higgle, and they'd gone about it in an extraordinarily complex manner.

"Marius is calling the gendarmes. We should all stay together and wait for them to arrive without too much discussion," I said, scanning the group for signs that anyone was on the cusp of doing something unpredictable... or looked calmer than expected.

"Is the party not happening?" Derek asked, frowning and looking confused about how he'd ended up here and what was going on.

"Not to worry! We'll have it another time," Damien said, trying to be nice and saying something equally strange.

"Perhaps you should all go back to the house and wait there?" I suggested, realising the open door to the barn with its distracting pool of blood and protruding body parts was not having a positive effect on anyone. The gendarmes might be less than thrilled that their witnesses would have had a chance to confer, but a scientifically perfect approach is not always the most humane one. I recognised a group of people who desperately needed to comfort each other somewhere that they felt secure. In any case, if one of them said something suspicious whilst they were in Damien's house, I was sure that it would be remembered. It was too bad I couldn't be there to listen personally, but I needed to get a closer look at something.

"I'll be with you in a second," I told Damien when he shot me a questioning look. "You should probably make some tea," I added, citing the British cure-all.

"Right, yes… that will make it better," he agreed, back on solid ground with that suggestion.

I waited until I was sure that the entire group had trooped off towards the house, before I braced myself and walked back into the barn. A glance at the compacted dirt floor told me that there would be no traces of footprints, so further walking wasn't going to destroy anything.

My gaze followed the cable again, all the way up to the rafters, where the small network of pulley systems began. I followed the line until it became a single one that ran down one of the central support struts of the barn that separated the mezzanine hayloft from the space below. A small, plastic box was stuck to the wooden bars of the loft. I could see a green light flashing on and off behind the translucent cover, which made me think it contained some sort of technology. There was an ancient stepladder in the back corner of the barn that definitely hadn't been touched in years, judging by the accumulation of dust, so I brought it over and scaled it in order to avoid touching the hayloft ladder. Fingerprints were unfortunately not as easy to come by as police shows on TV often made out - especially as gloves are the first precaution a clever criminal takes - but you never knew. Unfortunately, I knew that the chances of the arm of law enforcement responsible for more serious crimes bothering to carry out even that basic procedure would probably be fifty-fifty. If their past efforts were anything to go by, they'd be having a good day if they remembered to remove and bag up the giant murder weapon.

I climbed the rickety ladder, thinking that there was probably a good reason why these steps had been left abandoned for so long, but I managed to make it to the top without incident. I was almost at eye level with the mysterious plastic contraption when there was a loud *FZZZZT!* A burn hole appeared in the box, before the flames spread, melting the rest of the plastic parts and causing non-combustible pieces to rain down onto the dirt below.

"Fluff on a stick!" I cursed, briefly wondering if I had inadvertently caused vital evidence to explode, before common sense took hold again and I realised that I was standing on a ladder in a very old, very dry barn, that was little more than kindling for any uncontrolled open flame.

With surprising athleticism that I wish someone had been around to witness, I jumped down from the stepladder and ran over to the buffet table that was destined to never be picked over by hungry guests. An industrial sized carton of orange juice had been placed on one end. I tore it open, running back towards the flames that were flickering dangerously close to the loose hay that was still up in the loft, unswept from times long passed, when the farm had been a working one. The orange juice sloshed over the burning plastic, the glow fading, until only the acrid stench of burned plastic and spilled orange juice remained.

"I've called the gendarmes and told them how stringently we avoided any contamination or touching… what... what are you doing?!" Marius asked, grinding to a halt when he chose exactly the wrong moment to return to the barn.

"Ah," I said, looking at the now empty orange juice carton in my hand. "There is a logical explanation for all of this."

Marius sighed and looked resigned - a sign that we'd been through far too much of this sort of thing together. "I'm sure there is."

"It was a plastic control box that ignited as soon as I got close to it. I believe there was probably a timer mechanism inside that was designed to combust a certain amount of time after the trap had been sprung. Perhaps the person responsible had hoped it would burn the barn down, destroying all the evidence... only, we must have arrived earlier than they'd anticipated," I hypothesised, thinking about how no one had seemed too keen to go and find Fern when she hadn't materialised. I'd put it down to the others not wanting to be roped in to help out, but now it was framed in a different light.

"The gendarmes are not going to be pleased," Marius said, not looking too cut up about it. "I'm starting to think I should have a direct line to them. They're lucky I managed to find enough signal to get through."

"Everyone is back at the house. I put Damien in charge." I informed him, starting the long walk back across the field.

"What could possibly go wrong with Damien in charge?" Marius said sarcastically, shaking his head and looking quietly furious. "I've told him so many times! Weapons are bad news, and now look what's happened."

"Damien would undoubtedly point out that it's the people *using* the weapons who cause the problems," I countered.

"But if there weren't so many deadly items in easy reach..."

"...then anyone wishing to cause harm would undoubtedly find another method to achieve the same result," I finished for him, trying to keep things good-natured. As much as Marius liked to put the blame on Damien, so far, the man had never been proven guilty of any crime - beyond the accidental injury of a delivery man, but that had been cleared up. Yet again, the evidence before us suggested that he really should keep a closer eye on his weapons, but there was no actual law that kept you from owning an ancient armoury. It was using it that came with problems attached.

I resolved to keep an open mind about everyone present. The scene of the crime was etched in my mind, but without knowing anything more about Fern and the rest of the group than what I'd been able to glean during our first meeting, I had no way of pulling the answer from thin air. Perhaps the gendarmes would find something more whenever they deigned to turn up and take a closer look at the crime scene.

But not too close that they would query the unusual presence of orange juice in the remains of an electrical fire.

I was definitely going to have to do some explaining about that.

"Ah, Justine… just the person we all wanted to see," Damien greeted me when I returned to the house with Marius scuffing his feet along the ground behind me.

"Damien - just the man we'd like to ask a few questions," I replied, indicating that we should go into the kitchen to talk.

He shot a concerned glance over his shoulder in the direction of the other guests once the three of us were alone in his kitchen. "Questions? About what? I am heartbroken over poor Fern, but you said it wasn't my fault, didn't you?"

"*I* said nothing of the sort," Marius grumbled.

I ignored him. "Could you tell us more about the weapon that was used to kill Fern? For example… what exactly is it, and why was someone able to take it without you noticing and use it to murder your friend?" I could have phrased it all more delicately, but this wasn't exactly Damien's first rodeo. Or even his second, come to think of it. The man needed to swap his name labels for tracking devices.

"Ah, well… it's a halberd, which is an incredibly interesting weapon. There's not much documented about their specific use during battle. We know they were used in formation, but beyond that, the actual technique is a bit of a mystery - a fascinating one! Did you know, a halberd was responsible for the death of a 15th century duke? Charles The Bold found death on the end of one. I must admit, I was so excited about having the opportunity to buy one of the things, I rather forgot to account for its size. It was hard to find a place for it in here. I was going to get around to sticking it up on a wall, one of these days, but... until that time, I put it into storage."

"In a rickety old barn. How very safe and secure!" Marius said, filling his voice with sarcasm.

"You know there's next to no crime around here!" Damien protested, before hastily clearing his throat. "That is - apart from a few recent problems that are normally few and far between. All solved because of your excellent work," he added, remembering Marius' job and having a bash at throwing a compliment his way.

"The 'few' crimes we have around here always seem to have something to do with you. You're a facilitator," Marius accused him, unhappy about Damien's implication that his job was easy and basically a waste of time - even though we all knew that Marius did in fact spend most of his time chasing after escaped chickens and refereeing turf wars between farmers.

"Well, uh... I must be... making more tea," Damien said, dashing away to another corner of the kitchen to try and look busy.

"I can't believe this," Marius muttered when I led him into the other room. "I only came here today because I wanted to tell you how much I didn't enjoy it and to find out about all of the illegal things these foreigners are up to. There's always something underhand going on in groups like this," he said - making me uncertain whether he classed the murder as 'underhand', or if that fell under a different category of crime.

"Yes, I heard the baked bean blackmarket has exploded in the wake of Brexit," I said, rolling my eyes when Marius took me seriously and suddenly looked keen. "I knew I shouldn't have asked you to come," I muttered back, annoyed by Marius' behaviour. I'd known he wasn't too keen on Damien, and by extension, his friends... but I'd hoped he'd be open-minded enough to judge people after he met them. Admittedly, one of these people was probably a murderer, so I should probably cut him some slack in the judging department.

"How long are you going to keep us all here?" Ursula called towards us from the huddle of conversing Brits, and I hastily translated for Marius' benefit.

"The gendarmes are on their way," Marius said to reassure them - at least proving he could still behave professionally in front of people who weren't me. "You're all remaining here because it's important that the crime scene remains free from any further tampering that may influence the investigation. The person responsible can't be given the chance to sabotage any evidence they may have left behind."

"Hang on, are you trying to say that you think it's one of us who did it?" Derek asked after I'd translated that back, looking more shocked than he had done when we'd collectively found Fern.

"Did Fern have any enemies that any of you know of?" I asked, hoping to defuse the tension. The room fell silent as everyone looked towards Alex once again.

"No, I mean... I can't think of anything. It's all so melodramatic, having enemies and all that. Who really has enemies these days? I suppose you want me to think of anyone she might have fallen out with or offended, but..." Alex shook his head "...nothing springs to mind. We're just normal people with normal lives. We were," he added with a frown, struggling with the past tense.

"The spouse or boyfriend is usually the one who did it," Lyra said, stirring the cup of tea she was holding. She looked up and realised the focus was now on her, and Alex was white as a sheet. "Oh! I'm just saying that statistically speaking, in true crime…" She trailed off. "Not always, though. I mean, most of the really interesting crimes are committed by very unexpected people - which is why they end up on television."

"I don't think it's helpful for us to be pointing fingers at one another. When the gendarmes get here, they'll sow enough seeds of division on their own without needing our help to do it," Ursula said, giving her head a single shake.

Damien chose that moment to return to the room and took the opportunity to change the subject. "I told you all that Justine's a therapist, didn't I? After today, you may have a few more clients on your books," he said to me, trying to find the silver lining in a moment where it probably couldn't exist.

"I, uh…" I faltered, knowing I couldn't ethically take on clients who were undoubtedly going to be investigated over this murder - especially when I was also a witness.

"Maybe she killed Fern to get herself some more business," Henry suggested, rubbing his sideburns thoughtfully.

"Business is going well enough for Justine that she doesn't have to resort to murder in order to recruit new clients," Marius said, surprising me by coming to my defence so strongly and also understanding without the need for translation.

"I see she's also charmed the police enough for them to be biased in her favour," Henry continued, doing some translating of his own and speaking as if Marius and I weren't in the room listening to everything he was saying.

Fortunately, before Marius could forcibly stuff the Big Ben tea caddy down his throat, we were interrupted by a knock on the door.

After Damien answered it, gendarmes strode into the room without a word of greeting.

They ground to a halt when they saw the weapons that coated the walls, and then the lead gendarme's eyes found mine.

"You again!" he said, before buttoning his lips when he probably realised it was hardly a professional greeting. He had brown hair that was neatly side-parted in a more classic style than Marius' trendy long on top, short on the sides chop, and his eyes were like a pan of caramel that's just starting to burn. I recognised him as being part of the team who'd investigated the skeletons beneath my floor, but he hadn't been in charge back then.

"Yes… me again," I said, not seeing a better way to respond. It was, after all, the truth. Yet again, I'd got myself wrapped up in a crime, but also yet again, I was not responsible for the crime in question. Convincing the gendarmes of that would be a different matter altogether.

"I'm Marius Bisset, local chief of police," Marius said, stepping in front of the gendarme when he stared at me for far too long without saying anything else. "I've secured the scene, although, there was an unavoidable incident that I should tell you about…" He attempted to lead the gendarmes outside again, but their leader ignored him, still fixated on me - like he was trying to see inside my brain.

"I'm Jaques Laurent, captain of the Guéret gendarmerie. I will be in charge of this investigation," he said, seeming to direct every word exclusively at me. "Everyone must remain here in this building until my colleagues have interviewed you, taken your statements, and collected your contact details. Only then will you be permitted to leave," he finished, breaking off the intense moment and frowning at the hoard of embarrassingly British branded products that had been left on the table.

"Why are you here?" he said, turning back to me and speaking like there was nobody else present,

"It's Damien's surprise birthday party," I said, indicating the host, who currently seemed torn between excitement over the prospect of having a thrilling tale of adventure to tell dinner guests in the future, and horror over what had befallen one of his guests - which might make future dinner parties less inviting to others.

Jaques' eyebrows may have risen a little, but he didn't make any comments about the 'surprise' part not being the party itself. "Everyone stay here. Apart from you... and Monsieur Bisset, of course," he added - but it was very definitely an afterthought.

"Why her?" Marius asked, frowning and looking like he had a thing or two to say about the regional branch of police's methods of working.

Jaques blinked and gave him a cursory glance. "Because I said so," he said, dismissing the other man. "Oh, before I forget... no one is permitted to disclose any details of what you witnessed here today, until given consent. From the information we've been given, this is likely to become a murder investigation, and anyone found hindering the investigation will be charged with obstruction of justice. The last thing we need is for small town gossips to stick their noses in..." And with that final warning, he walked back out of the house.

Marius' face underwent a curious display of changing expressions, before finally fixing on a thunderously dark one that threatened imminent explosion.

"He's rather handsome for a gendarme, isn't he?" Lyra said in a carrying voice, seemingly not caring that the rest of us could hear her thoughts and that the other gendarmes were also listening in.

Perhaps Marius really did understand more English than he was letting on, because he looked even more furious when he left the house in pursuit of the other man.

I wasn't sure that solving the murder was the first thing on his mind.

4

PICNICS AND POLICE

"I expected you back later!" Marissa said, looking up from her book in surprise when I walked into my living room in the final hours of the afternoon. She hastily stuffed the *Mills and Boon* novel she'd been reading behind a cushion, even as I raised an eyebrow at her. "Oh, I suppose I shouldn't be ashamed of enjoying a bit of romance once in a while."

I raised the other eyebrow.

She cleared her throat. "Well, romance and… other things. Damien's parties usually go on late into the night. I was sure you wouldn't be home until at least gone twelve!" Spice looked up from his place on the sofa and tilted his head at me, seeming to say that he wouldn't have minded if I'd been gone for longer. Marissa was a soft touch when it came to treats.

"Something happened," I said, hoping to keep things vague.

"Something like…?" Marissa pressed, wanting to know more detail. I should have been expecting it. The post-mistress prided herself in knowing all of the town's gossip, and she was also responsible for doing a fair bit of spreading it around.

I sighed, knowing that she would kill me if she heard about what had happened at Damien's party from someone else, but mindful of the gendarme's words of warning. His very specific words, now that I thought about it. It was almost as if he remembered Marissa from the last murder. Jaques' face popped into my mind when I thought about him. I blinked to get it to go away again - only slightly regretful that I couldn't dwell on his remarkable jawline just a little longer. "The gendarmes told all of us that we're not allowed to say anything..." I began, seeing a pathway through this that didn't involve me sharing details.

"The gendarmes are involved? They asked you not to say anything?" Marissa repeated, her mouth turning into a perfect 'o'. "Something serious must have happened... a crime that they want you to keep quiet about because it might affect their evidence gathering." She glanced at me for confirmation. I studiously avoided making eye contact, but also didn't deny anything. "Wait - is someone dead in an unnatural causes sort of way?"

I took a deep breath and continued to study the ceiling.

"Come on, Justine! You can't do this to me! It's not Damien, is it? Has someone killed him? That seems hard to believe. The only person who vocally doesn't like the old stick is Marius, and he was... well, he was with you."

I stopped studying the ceiling long enough to shoot her a look which conveyed that I knew she was deliberately baiting me. You can't out psych a psychologist. "Damien is fine and Marius hasn't murdered anyone." *Yet*, I silently added in my head, thinking both Damien and Jaques Laurent would need to tread carefully in the near future.

"But someone *did* murder someone else," Marissa guessed, rubbing her chin and going all thoughtful. "Damien always spends his birthday with a group of expats. He never invites anyone from around here to that event. I believe they just speak English the whole time, and he's considerate of things like that," she said, not surprising me by being in the know about Damien's affairs. "That means it's probably one of them who's dead... and one of them who did the killing - if it was committed by someone close to the victim, which most murders are. Unless it was an accidental death?" she tacked on, remembering that accidents were still something the gendarmes would be involved in and could ask for the silence of the witnesses, so the next of kin could be notified first.

I sighed again, almost feeling like the spectre of Jaques Laurent was glaring at me through the window, watching my every move. "It wasn't accidental," I said, wondering if that counted as breaking the silence I'd promised to keep. I decided it rather depended on how you looked at it, but if the gendarme had been eavesdropping right this second, I doubted he would be pleased. "You can't say anything to anyone," I told Marissa. "Not until it's officially announced."

Marissa sat back in her chair, a frown knitting her brows together. She fiddled with the decorative knot on the end of her chunky, gold necklace. "I couldn't possibly say anything to anyone when I don't know any of the details! I almost wish I hadn't pressured you to tell me anything at all, if that's the most you can hint at. Almost," she added when I opened my mouth to say I wished I hadn't said anything either. "I bet it's something really dramatic, isn't it?"

I looked towards the window, seeking an escape.

"What was it... decapitation by sword? Stabbed many times by ninja throwing stars - or whatever the medieval equivalent of that is?"

"Marissa!" I protested.

"Blown up by a bomb in a birthday cake? Now that would

be a good way to go. That is, people would be talking about it forever," the postmistress continued, enjoying her theories every bit as much as she would have enjoyed hearing the truth.

The landline ringing made me jump, showing that I was still on edge. "Stop guessing!" I implored Marissa, who looked like she was concocting several hundred more theories - all based off her knowledge of Damien's weapon collection. "Hello?" I said, answering the phone and shooting glares at the postmistress, who was having way too much fun.

"Justine, it's Jaques Laurent," the resonant voice on the other end of the line said.

I fumbled the phone several times before catching it again. This was just a coincidence and the man calling me did not have some sort of psychic sense that warned him when someone was close to spilling secrets about crime scenes. "What can I do for you?" I asked, pressing my finger to my lips and sending death glares at Marissa - who might start loudly popping off more theories at any moment.

"It's more what I can do for you. I was just calling to check that you're doing okay after..." He cleared his throat. "Most people find it very distressing to see what you saw today, and I know it was asking a lot to have you return to the scene of the crime and recap everything that had transpired."

I raised an eyebrow. He meant most people - except for the person who'd committed the crime - would find it distressing. This was probably less of a caring courtesy call and more of a subtle segue into hunting for suspects. "I'm sure you're already aware that I have the dubious benefit of having more experience than most with crime scenes," I said, knowing that honesty was normally the best policy. "However, it was certainly not pleasant," I added in that trademark British way of understating something that was awful, whilst exaggerating almost everything else. Bad traffic was an absolute nightmare, but if the Crown Jewels were ever stolen, the incident would likely be described as a spot of bother.

There was a pause as he waited to see if I was going to elaborate, or be overcome by emotion… and I waited to see why he was really calling.

"Well, I'm glad you're doing all right. If there's anything you need, I gave you a card with my contact details on, didn't I?" he said, breaking first. No one could out wait a therapist.

"You did, and I will… thank you," I said, and was semi-surprised when he wished me a good evening and put the phone down - probably adding a question mark next to my name. I shook my head, knowing that if I was currently on the list of possible suspects, it wouldn't be for long. I had absolutely no connection to the woman who'd died, beyond us being from the same country.

"Who was that?" Marissa asked with a twinkle in her eye.

"No one important. I mean, it was the gendarme who's in charge of the… thing," I said, hastily changing the end of my sentence.

"Why is he calling you? Didn't you only see him a short while ago?" Marissa was annoyingly perceptive when she wanted to be. It was one of the reasons why she was so good at rooting out all of the best gossip.

"I'm sure he's calling everyone who was there to check up on their state of mind and see if anyone is taking it too well, or has gone completely the other way," I added, knowing how it was easy to overcompensate if you had something to hide.

"Does this gendarme speak enough English to be understood when asking his questions? Damien gave me the impression that his friends were all diehard English speakers who would no sooner learn French than give up their tea addiction."

"I'm not sure," I said, suddenly wondering if I was right about Jaques calling everyone else, and also how well his team had done collecting statements today. "I know some of them speak a bit of French," I added, thinking back to the party.

"Maybe he's already picked you out as someone suspicious," Marissa half-joked. "Hang on… what does he look like? How old is he?" she asked, squinting at my cheeks, which were probably turning pink. "Ooh, so he's not ugly!"

"No, he is not ugly, but what he is, is the person investigating this… incident. Hopefully he will do a better job than the captain before him."

Marissa shrugged. "I don't know… you and Marius have done just fine sorting this kind of thing out before."

"Yes, but that's not the way things should be," I reminded her.

"Well, we'll see." A mischievous smile danced on Marissa's lips. "It's almost tempting to commit a serious crime, just to get a closer look…"

"Stop it. I'm sure he will be very focused on this new case. As a potential suspect myself, I doubt there will be any relationship between us beyond the professional kind."

"Does that mean you would be interested in something beyond professional, if it were to happen?" Marissa probed, doing a good job of getting more than I wanted to say out of me.

"Today is the first time we've ever spoken. We're not getting married. Now, shoo… there are things I should probably be getting on with, seeing as the party was cancelled," I told her, wondering what things in particular I was thinking of doing. The truth was, I didn't want to tell Marissa anything more than had already slipped out about the murder, and this new topic of conversation also wasn't doing me any favours.

"Okay, I'm going! And just for you, I'll keep quiet about everything you didn't tell me until it's officially allowed to be spoken about, but the minute you know more, and can say more…"

"I'll call you," I promised, knowing that there was nothing Marissa hated more than hearing secondhand gossip.

"Good. I've trained you well," my friend said, flashing me a wicked grin on her way to the door. "Have a good evening. You also have to tell me if that nice gendarme calls again."

"No I don't," I told her with an evil smile of my own, gently shutting the front door behind her. I loved Marissa dearly, but telling her anything to do with my love life (which, rather disappointingly, didn't actually exist) was a recipe for becoming the town's new hot gossip topic.

* * *

I was sipping tea in the living room the next morning, still blinking the sleep from my eyes, when there was a knock on the door. My heart pounded for a moment as I wondered if it was the gendarmes (and maybe one of them in particular) visiting for a very early questioning session. I looked down at my fluffy pink dressing gown decorated with hearts, and didn't even have to reach up to know I was currently sporting a bird's nest of curls on my head. Hair like mine needed some serious taming before being allowed out in public.

"Oh, get real," I muttered, stalking to the door, whilst reminding myself very firmly that this was not a dating opportunity. Viable options may be few and far between, but I was not going to fling myself at anyone with a pretty face, who wasn't pushing eighty years of age, out of desperation. I lived a perfectly lovely life without a partner, and I was happy. It didn't matter how I looked to the person standing on my doorstep at this far too early hour.

But the visitor standing behind my newly installed oak front door was not Jaques Laurent.

I frowned as the previous day's events swam before me for a moment. "Hello, Ursula. What can I do for you?" I asked the woman standing on my doorstep. *And how did you find out where I live?* I silently wondered, before answering my own question a second later - Damien. He must have decided to push the therapy recommendations, even after I'd explained why I couldn't ethically provide any assistance.

"It's Justine, isn't it?" she said, even though she obviously knew exactly who I was, having decided to make the trip to meet me again. "I thought I would come to see if you're okay after yesterday. We Brits should stick together," she added, not very convincingly.

I didn't draw attention to the obvious flaw in that statement - which was that sticking together with Brits had possibly been a factor in Fern's death. "I'm fine, thank you. I feel terrible about what happened to Fern, but I didn't ever get to meet her, unlike the rest of you. I'm sure you must be devastated," I said, wondering if I was pushing things along in the right direction.

Ursula nodded and her eyes grew watery on cue. "Yes, it was really hard. I mean, things have been stressful enough recently with Derek, but what happened to Fern is more than I can handle right now. I don't think I can do it all anymore, you know?" she said, looking up at me with her eyes miraculously dry again to see if her words were having any effect.

"Why don't you come in for a cup of tea?" I suggested, knowing that resistance was largely futile when it came to people seeking to talk - even though I'd drawn my line in the sand when it came to not being able to take on any clients from this group.

"Do you have Earl Grey?" Ursula asked, breezing past wearing a tailored linen blazer over a thin silk blouse, that had probably cost more than the price my house would currently be valued at. She looked around with the air of someone distinctly used to more salubrious surroundings (mine were currently more of a work in progress) before making her way straight into the living room, which currently remained the most completed room of the house.

I allowed myself one single head shake, before I put the kettle on again and rooted around for something in my cupboard that may have been Earl Grey once upon a time. I looked at the bag I pulled out dubiously, vaguely remembering having seen the box when I'd moved into the property I'd won in a raffle. Could tea go bad? I reflected that the answer was undoubtedly yes, but perhaps I could call this 'aged' and get away with it.

And perhaps terrible tea will be enough to persuade her not to come back! a rebellious voice whispered in my head, making me feel guilty for a second, before I remembered that Ursula not returning was indeed the outcome I wanted.

"Here you are," I said, setting the bright pink mug down on the table in front of Ursula - who gave it a cursory glance and then proceeded to ignore my offering, which was probably for the best.

"It feels strange being here and talking to a total stranger about these things, but Damien said you were very good, and frankly, I'm desperate. There's no one around here I can talk to, even if I could do it all in the lingo." She sighed and waved a hand, apparently assuming that, as a therapist, I was just here to talk to anyone about anything, and at any time they pleased. I prided myself in being as accepting of humans and their nature as possible, but Ursula was a particularly prickly example.

"I'm listening," I said - knowing that she would have carried on talking regardless.

"Fern dying brought it all home for me. That's what happens with a sudden death, isn't it? It makes you reevaluate the path you're on in life."

I tilted my head but remained silent, privately thinking that not everyone viewed sudden death as a personal sign, but it was quite clear that Ursula was someone who believed that the world revolved around her.

"That's when I really got to thinking about my marriage," she said, somehow managing to gift the word 'marriage' an extra syllable.

"Are you concerned about your relationship?" I asked, summoning the memory of Ursula's husband Derek. Next to Ursula, he seemed to be a sparrow cosying up to a peacock, but appearances didn't always matter. When it came to love, it was what lay inside that counted in the long term.

"Of course I am, but then… doesn't everyone wonder from time to time if they've made a terrible mistake in their choice of partner and have wasted half their life with the wrong man?" A slightly crazed laugh escaped her lips before her unruffled exterior returned. "It just got me thinking, that's all." Her eyes seemed to focus on the pink mug, but I got the impression that she was seeing something else. "Speaking of romance gone wrong… do you think the gendarmes will be investigating Alex? Lyra seemed to think that they would."

"I think they'll be investigating everyone," I replied as diplomatically as possible.

She nodded. "Obviously… but, would they search the apartment where they lived together, or anything like that?"

I inwardly raised an eyebrow at this rather specific

enquiry. "It's possible. I'm sure the gendarmes are keeping an open mind about everything at this early stage. They'll be gathering as much potential evidence as they can - which may include going through Fern's things to find out if she has anything in her possession that may give a clue as to why someone might have wanted her dead," I said, knowing I wasn't exactly confiding some big secret when that was standard protocol.

"I see. You're probably right about that," Ursula said with a sigh, rising to her feet. "I must be off. I've been here far too long already," she added, implying that I was the one twisting her arm to stick around. "Book me in for therapy biweekly. Tuesdays and Fridays are good for me."

"What would you hope to achieve by having therapy?" I asked out of curiosity.

"I want to be my best self. I find it very hard to make decisions, you know. I'm just not forceful enough - that's my problem."

It took all of my psychotherapist training to stop my eyebrows from shooting up into my hairline.

"I'll bring Derek, too. Maybe you can fix him for me," she added as an afterthought.

"I'm afraid I can't take on you, or anyone else who was at Damien's surprise birthday party, as therapy clients. I offer all my clients confidentiality, and that's something I can't do, due to the current situation." - Meaning that if anyone told me anything juicy, I'd have to whisper it straight into the ear of Jaques Laurent.

"Surely you can make an exception? I'll pay whatever," Ursula said - apparently also someone who was used to money being able to open every single door.

"I'm afraid I can't," I replied, holding firm but keeping a polite smile on my face.

She shot me a disbelieving look, before walking swiftly

back to the front door with me trotting along behind in an effort to keep up. "Oh, I almost forgot… I'm supposed to invite you to Damien's get-together today. It's a picnic in a field. We always do it the day after his birthday. He normally puts it on as a thank you - where he does the food in return for what we did for him the day before. He often lacks some of the essentials from home that really make a picnic a picnic, which is why we started helping him out by gifting him hampers of food from England." A flash of nostalgia entered her eyes for a moment, whilst I silently wondered if Damien was aware that he was the architect of his own unwanted gifts. "Of course, this year will be a bit different, but it will still be nice."

"Different… because Fern has been murdered?" I asked, wanting to get that much clear.

"Well, yes… but now you're here to make up the numbers, which is handy, isn't it? It's at one o' clock. I'll tell Damien you're coming. Toodle-oo!"

I seized the door just as she was trying to close it on her way out. *Not forceful enough indeed!* I silently thought, as I fought with both the will of the other woman and the strength of her manicured hands. "The gendarmes won't approve of the same group of people who witnessed yesterday's incident meeting and discussing it. We were all warned to stay silent!"

A look of surprise jumped onto Ursula's face. "This doesn't really count though, does it? We've always spent this day together, so surely it falls under going about your lives as you normally would."

"Did the gendarmes say we should do that?" I asked, knowing that they hadn't.

"Well, I'm sure that's what they would have said if they'd stopped to consider the amount of distress this has caused all of us." Ursula waved a hand to shoo away any doubts. "In any case, we'll be together. All of us! It's not as if anything is going to happen. There's not even any proof that one of us did it, is there? Fern had a life outside of our little group. Perhaps she had a secret life." She arched a dark blonde eyebrow, inviting me to fill in the gaps however I chose. "You should come today, and come on your own. I don't know what's going on between you and your grumpy friend, but don't let him get in the way of you socialising with new and interesting people," Ursula said - as though she was the one qualified to give life advice.

"I see," I replied, truly seeing that Ursula did not want Sellenoise's one and only police agent spoiling the picnic party by doing the sensible thing and banning it before it could begin.

"It's sorted then. I'll ping you the location an hour before we meet," she said, wiggling her fingers at me and managing to slip through the doorway. "Just between us, remember!" she added over her shoulder when she was getting back into her car, trying to sparkle and make this picnic party seem like it was a worthwhile act of rebellion - instead of a self-serving social event where gossip would undoubtedly fly, like wasps around a patisserie stall.

I bit my lip, chewing over the problematic picnic. I wondered what Damien was thinking, taking part in it, and decided his weakness for human company had probably let him down this time. That much, I could understand and forgive - especially when he lived alone. It was the motives of the others that remained murky.

"Oh, bother," I said out loud, weighing up my options. I could completely ignore the invitation and keep my nose as clean and shiny as Rudolph's. On the other hand, I could simply report the picnic to Monsieur Laurent, earning myself brownie points with him and probably putting a stop to the ill-advised gathering. The downside of that option was that the crime of attending a picnic was unlikely to get anyone arrested and conveniently removed from daily life (even if it broke the rules stated by Jaques) - which meant that I could risk making myself public enemy number one to the killer.

What's the worst that can happen at a picnic? I thought, reassuring myself that I was only going there for damage control, and I might be able to do some good if I went…. like looking out for anything unusual or suspicious. Plus, if someone like Marius or Jaques were to complain about the lack of reporting from me, I could fudge things a bit and tell them that I'd only been made aware of the event just prior to its start.

I sighed and moved a hand up to my mouth to bite my nails, before lowering it again, knowing my excuses were far from the work of a genius.

My thoughts were interrupted by my laptop pinging to let me know that I had a new email. I walked over and clicked on the alert.

Bonjour Justine,

I am writing to ask if you are still doing well. Could we meet later today? There is something important I would like to talk to you about.

I would appreciate it if you could keep our correspondence private, as it concerns the investigation.

Regards,

Jaques Laurent

I managed to stop my heart from jumping out from my chest as it pounded for the second time this morning, before I told myself to calm down. Jaques was not watching me, and this was a total coincidence. Hardly a coincidence, really - given that there had been a murder yesterday, and he was in charge of investigating it. He'd probably been doing background checks and had got to mine and found something that he wanted explained. The disarming tone of the email was probably contrived to lull me into a false sense of security, so when we met for the surprise interrogation, my guard would be down.

Or perhaps someone else had told him about the picnic, and I was walking into a trap.

I sighed, knowing that I was already in too deep. What was one more misdemeanour? Especially when it came accompanied with free food - which just happened to be my favourite kind.

5

GETTING AWAY WITH MURDER

Even though Ursula had told me to come alone, I did bring along one uninvited guest.

"It's Damien - he always has more food than necessary," I said to my companion, who tilted his head at me and looked unsure. "In any case, you're excellent at wrapping everyone around your paw," I told Spice, who perked up at that pronouncement, or perhaps it was the sight of the field with a large oak tree at the centre of an ocean of golden wheat - a shady island in the midst of the August heat.

"Justine! Come on over! The others are just getting a few things out of my car for me," Damien called out when he saw me waiting by the gate. "My farmer friend always allows me to use this field for my annual post-party picnic. You can let your dog off his lead, I'm sure the wheat is safe from him."

"I'm not sure if the food will be," I joked back.

Damien laughed, but it sounded far less merry than usual. He was trying hard to appear as though he was enjoying himself, because being the warm and welcoming host was what he excelled at. I also mentally confirmed my earlier suspicion that the reason the ill-advised picnic had gone ahead was because Damien needed it far more than the people he was putting it on for. His greatest strength was his ability to connect with others, but without them, I sensed he was lost living out in the sticks with only Orwell the cat for company. I also understood that, with Monsieur Laurent banning us from talking about the ongoing investigation with others, Damien had probably decided that the only way he could get around that rule - or at least, bend it - was to remain in the company of those who'd witnessed the same events, so at least he had someone to talk to in order to feel like himself again. Grief was hard for everyone, but it was even more challenging to face it alone.

"Did you see my car when you arrived - the beautiful red MG Midget? I've had it in my garage for years in bits, waiting for a spare moment to fix it up," Damien said with an eye roll at his own expense, "but Henry dropped round recently and fixed it all without me even knowing he was there. He's quite the mechanical genius!"

"Is he?" I said, my interest piqued.

Damien waved a hand. "Oh, come on now... I know the way your mind works. I just meant in a manner of speaking. He's not one of the ones around here with a degree in engineering."

Whilst Spice ran back and forth chasing butterflies, Damien and I sipped a very civilised gin cocktail he'd brought with him in a thermos to keep it cold, before serving it in some proper balloon glasses. This picnic was certainly a far cry from foil-wrapped sandwiches. The moment after I had the thought, Damien cast a careful look around and produced something wrapped in foil from the small bag he had with him.

"Just for you, Justine... because I know you will appreciate it."

I looked down at a handful of toasted baguette slices, pre-spread with a marvellous looking pâte .

"I'm afraid this is as good as it will get today. The rest is all cold quiche and cheddar. I did try to convince them to sample our local delicacies, but they like what they like," Damien explained, sighing lightly as the rest of the group could be heard bickering over something behind the hedge. "You must be thinking that this get-together is a terrible idea, but the reason I went ahead with it is because I know that some of our number struggle to feel at home here in France, and losing a friend just makes that feeling worse. I know so many people who moved out here and then discovered what it feels like to not fit in somewhere for the first time in their lives. So many of them need…" he hesitated "…well, I suppose they need someone like you to talk to, but that's out of the question now, isn't it?"

"It is," I confirmed, hoping that would put an end to him handing out my address to anyone else - especially any potential murderers. "The captain of the gendarmes wants to speak with me this afternoon, although I haven't confirmed a time with him." Mostly because my guilty conscience said that if I pretended I hadn't received the email, then I wouldn't have missed an opportunity to come clean about the picnic prior to it occurring.

"Really? No one has been in touch with me since yesterday. They stayed behind after everyone had left and asked me a few more questions, but that was it," Damien said, looking surprised. I was relieved when he didn't dwell on it further. "I expect they're doing some checking up on all of us before returning with the next round of queries. Did you notice anything that might help solve the case?" Damien asked, his eyes begging me to say that everything would be wrapped up easily, and in such a way that it would miraculously avoid ripping up his social circle.

I opened my mouth to reply with something vague, but Damien kept talking.

"And before you remind me that it was one of my weapons that was used, I just want to say that I really regret it - of course I do - but I wish people would respect their purpose. Their true purpose!"

I waited.

"History!" he said, exasperated that I hadn't given him the answer he clearly believed was obvious.

"This is some really lovely pâté," I said, knowing that at least when it came to food we shared the same opinion.

"Yes, it is, isn't it? You know... I do wonder about this group sometimes... what it was that brought us all here. Nobody likes to admit it, but when they start a new life it's usually because there's something in the old one that they wanted to leave behind. Fern was no different from the rest of us in that respect. She wanted to forget her past, but I can't help wondering if she ever told me the whole story about what happened. Oh! We'd better finish up. The rabble are back," he added, easily diverted in the face of more socialising.

I spared a moment to scrutinise Damien, wondering if he was putting on a facade in front of his friends. I knew the answer was undoubtedly yes, and that he was concealing his true feelings right now. The question was... were those feelings merely grief, or was he harbouring something darker behind his cheerful features? I shook the thought away as soon as I had it. Damien lived for socialising. The possibility that he would sabotage his own birthday party was even less likely than the possibility of him being a murderer.

The others returned and the food was doled out. I tried not to laugh at the sorry looking pork pies that had been shipped all the way from the UK, or quite possibly smuggled here in someone's suitcase - given the new regulations. Still, I was never one to say no to food, and it wasn't all that bad. By the time I'd eaten my third cocktail sausage and cold chicken nugget, I thought I might be missing grey skies and heavy puddings just as much as the rest of them.

"Has anyone else been hounded by the gendarmes?" Alex asked when everyone had finished their first plateful. He tried to say it in an offhand manner, but I could tell from his body language that he'd been shaken by whatever scrutiny he'd found himself subjected to.

"They visited us yesterday evening, but it was hard to understand what they were asking," Ursula confirmed, before the others all nodded and murmured that they too had been visited and bothered. I kept quiet, but observed that I had not experienced the same treatment as the other guests or Damien. It was logical, if you accepted that the motive for murder was likely to be a personal one. I hadn't been given the opportunity to form any kind of relationship with Fern. I wondered if Marius had been similarly excluded and made a mental note to ask him about it later.

I was fending Spice off from the cocktail sausages when my mobile phone let out a little tone to let me know it had received a text. There was something intriguing about the way that mobile phone signal could be zero in town, but if you wandered into a field in the middle of nowhere and happened to be in just the right place, at just the right time, you might be treated to a whole two bars. The rest of the world may be in the 21st century, but a lot of the 21st Century had yet to put in an appearance in Sellenoise and its surrounding areas. I'd always thought that was part of its charm... until I had to make a phone call, anyway.

I pulled my phone out and glanced at the screen, after throwing a few sausages across the field for Spice to hunt down.

. . .

Where are you?

I glanced at the number and matched it with the near-photographic image I had in my mind of the business card given to me by Jaques Laurent.

I took a breath and returned my phone to my pocket, cursing those modern 'read' notifications, which would mean that he was definitely going to know I was ignoring him. Perhaps I could tell him that I'd momentarily got signal and then lost it again before I could send a reply. I fiddled with the single pink pearl pendant I'd worn today, wondering again if I should be here looking for answers when the gendarmes appeared to be taking things more seriously this time around. Was it old habits dying hard, or did I miss getting involved in mysteries - like the ones I'd once helped to solve?

"How is life treating you all? We didn't get a chance to have a chinwag yesterday," Henry said, breaking the sombre silence that had descended over everyone in the wake of talking about the gendarmes. "Derek... what are you up to these days, you old stick? We never got into the details."

Derek winced at being referred to as 'old' when Henry was quite probably older than he was. Both men were doing what they could to cover that with hair dye - only, Derek had less of it to colour. "My kinetic sculptures are selling very well. I have an exhibition in Munich soon, and commissions come in from all across Europe."

"Amazing what people will buy," Henry said, shaking his head and looking awed.

"What about you, old boy?" Derek bit back. "I heard you're still doing odd jobs for expats. There can't be much money in that. We're not in the South of France!"

"You'd be surprised," Henry said, not letting Derek get under his skin in the slightest.

"I'm doing great," Lyra piped up. "The company is doing really well, and it looks like they're staying in Guéret for good."

"That's brilliant news!" Damien chimed in.

"I consider myself fortunate to have been given the opportunity. Plus, it's fun really, isn't it?" she said, glancing at Alex for backup.

"Work is work," he replied, not sounding anywhere near as enthusiastic as Lyra.

"What is it that you do exactly?" I asked, finding it interesting that it was this topic which so often acted as an icebreaker for Brits. In France, asking about a person's job when you didn't know each other was considered rude, because it led to an instantaneous judgement being made. Instead, it was far more common to ask where a person liked to go on holiday.

And then judge them based on that instead.

"I'm a mechanical engineer, specialising in the design of components for new tech. Put simply, if a tech company wants to build a machine that does a thing, we're the ones they come to in order to make it actually work," she explained, well used to having to translate her job into terms that others understood.

"I'm in international jewellery sales," Ursula said when the silence resumed after Lyra had spoken. "I get to travel quite a lot, which is good, because I'm not cut out for peace and quiet the way the person who thought we should move here is," she added with a sideways glare at her husband.

"I need silence and space for my work!" Derek protested.

I observed their bickering and reflected again that, on the surface, they seemed an unlikely couple. And yet… they must share something that had brought them together and kept them united. In some ways, it was too bad I couldn't offer them therapy, as I was curious to know what that magic ingredient might be.

"I'm a remote PA for fashion brand CEOs," Miranda announced, eyeing Ursula when she said it - the two women apparently believing they were vying for the position of most impressive job, when it was Lyra's that really interested me.

"You work doing engineer stuff, too, don't you Alex? You're with the same company that Lyra works for," Henry prompted when Fern's fiancé made no move to jump in with his own career.

"I don't engineer things. I just check the safety of what's built. I'm basically a troubleshooter," Alex replied, looking exceedingly unenthusiastic about this conversation.

"The gendarmes said to me that someone built a giant trap for Fern. Someone who works in engineering would be well qualified to pull off something like that," Derek said - apparently under the impression he was being subtle.

"Oh yeah? And your chain reaction creations don't fit perfectly with the modus operandi?" Alex practically exploded. "You're just trying to point the finger at me, so it doesn't get pointed at you. It's exactly what the killer would do!" A sausage roll was crushed to mush as his hand rolled into a fist.

"I'm terribly concerned that all of this is my fault," Damien interjected, causing everyone to turn and look at him, when he remarkably didn't appear to be accusing anyone else of anything. "I'm a bit of a bargain hunter when it comes to weaponry. I have my own set of strategies for getting the lowest price I can, and I do my research. It's not my fault when a seller doesn't know the true value of what they have, is it? There have been a few times when a seller has worked out an item's value after they'd already parted with it, and I have been accused of foxing them on the price."

He sighed. "I don't wish to make my enemies sound too dramatic, but a boobytrap with a halberd could be their idea of just deserts. I have been threatened before, but I never imagined they would actually take action… and what if a trap meant for me killed poor Fern instead?"

"Wouldn't it be more direct to come at you with a sword or throwing axe?" Derek pointed out, his large forehead furrowing as he contemplated this round the houses approach.

"Well, I don't know how the mind of a criminal works," Damien protested. "The point is… it could be my fault!"

"I don't think it was a disgruntled weapons seller," Lyra spoke up when Damien was so distressed that he even bit into a dry, very well travelled, sausage roll. "Anyone planning a complex trap wouldn't have built it in any old place, to spring at any old time. I'm afraid it's far more likely that the target was Fern. After all, everyone here knew she was going to be in that barn," she finished, before flashing me an apologetic look when she realised that wasn't strictly true. Out of everyone at the picnic today, I was the least likely to have murdered Fern… but I'd known that much already.

A heavy feeling hung over the picnic, like the static from an electrical storm that's about to hit, as everyone considered the people they were sitting next to.

My phone bleeped again, breaking the spell.

"You've got signal?" Ursula murmured. Right on cue, everyone pulled out their phones to check if they had it, too. It was what passed for an everyday thrill around here.

"Anyone important?" Damien asked - almost as eager as Marissa was to get his hands on some gossip.

"No, not really," I said, glancing at the new text from Jaques, which now said: 'I need to see you'. It definitely seemed more urgent than the previous message. It was probably time to make my escape from this prickly picnic before the sausage rolls started to fly. I typed out a quick reply whilst the signal remained.

Come to my house this evening, if convenient. If possible, please drive a plain car. I'd rather not alarm my neighbours after the last time.

I pressed send, before wondering if I should have brought up the skeletons I'd found beneath my floor when I was in the midst of another murder investigation.

My phone buzzed again.

"My, my... someone's popular!" Miranda said with a thick-lipped smile. She meant it jokingly, but I could tell that some others in the group were starting to wonder exactly who was texting me so much. It was yet another reason to not fall in with a clique. I didn't want to be unfriendly - I loved people and lived for being sociable, almost as much as Damien - but it was never good to be stuck in an insular friendship ring, who'd isolated themselves from everyone else. It tended to lead to bad things... things, like grisly murders.

Great. See you at 9 tonight. Looking forward to it.

I raised an eyebrow at the last part, but perhaps it was just Jaques' way of trying to show me how seriously he was taking the case this time around, having witnessed his gendarmerie's less than stellar work in the past. "I think it's time for me to go home. Thank you for everything, Damien," I said, smiling brightly at the eccentric man.

"Second time's the charm!" he replied, standing up and embracing me - congratulating himself on no one dying at the picnic.

"Where's the fire?" Derek joked, sharing a sideways look with Ursula.

"No fire," I told him with a thin smile. "I've just got a date with a gendarme."

I turned and walked away with Spice bouncing at my heels before the whispers could begin. Part of me wondered if I'd regret my tongue-in-cheek words, but a larger part of me had enjoyed putting the cat among the pigeons.

I moved quickly, but not quickly enough to be out of earshot when Derek commented: "That's one way to get away with murder."

6

A SINGULAR CELEBRATION

I'd just put the kettle on when I heard the sound of a car engine outside my house. A glance through the beautiful glass windows that surrounded my brand new front door revealed that Jaques had pulled up in a shiny black Mercedes Benz. It looked curiously out of place against the backdrop of abandoned farm machinery and piles of logs drying out for winter. There was a small flash as someone lifted a curtain in the fading twilight at the end of the long summer's day, before dropping it again. I was silently grateful that Jaques had taken my recommendation seriously about not turning up with his blue lights flashing. The last thing I needed was to start a fresh neighbourhood feud when the old one had only concluded recently.

"It's quite late really, isn't it?" I said to myself while I dithered around in the kitchen, wondering if I should stick with the mugs I'd got out for tea or coffee, or offer the gendarme something stronger. He probably couldn't drink on duty though, could he? Tea was almost certainly the right choice. I also had a tin of decent biscuits that I'd got out in case he wanted a snack.

Inwardly, I wondered if I should be offering him anything at all when he was surely here to interrogate me over my possible role in the death of Fern Higgle, but it felt rude to be standoffish in my own house. After all, he was doing me a big favour by coming here, when he could have demanded that I come to the gendarmerie. It was considerate of him… and mildly perplexing.

"Good evening, Justine. You don't mind if I call you Justine, do you?" Jaques said when I opened the door for him.

"Of course you can," I replied, noting his early attempt to disarm me by acting overfamiliar. It was textbook police work - although, I was surprised to see Jaques playing this softer role. On the surface, he came across as someone far more likely to be the type to handcuff a suspect to a chair and throw water at them until they talked.

"It should go without saying that you can call me Jaques." He smiled when I invited him in, little creases appearing around his golden brown eyes. I observed that he wasn't wearing his uniform and had instead come dressed in dark jeans and a tight black T-shirt. He might not be wearing anything emblazoned with badges, but anyone would be able to spot that he worked in law enforcement a mile off.

"What can I do for you?" I asked when we were sitting down. I'd offered him tea, and when he hadn't seemed keen, I'd taken a chance by mentioning wine and had been surprised when he'd accepted a glass. Now, we were on opposite sides of my kitchen table in the middle of a room that was still half a building site - but a building site that was bordering on being cool and chic, instead of derelict. "I assume this isn't a social call?" I added, hoping an attempt at light humour might help to ease the strange tension that had settled in the room after Jaques had sipped his wine and watched me without speaking.

"We do need to talk about Fern Higgle," he said with a

surprising amount of reluctance. This man was really committing to the friendly confidant style of questioning. "It's come to my attention that there was a meeting between witnesses today. Were you there?"

"I'm afraid I was," I confessed feeling extremely sheepish, but had I really expected it to remain a secret when there were so many gossips in the group? *And so much backstabbing,* I mentally added, remembering the fiery exchanges at the picnic. "I didn't mean to interfere with this case, but I thought it might be useful to be there to see if anyone said anything that might help your investigation. I was going to tell you about it," I added, feeling like a sneak.

Jaques sat back, but he wasn't looking at me in disbelief or disgust. "I don't suppose anything interesting did happen?"

I considered carefully. "Well, no one confessed," I said with my tongue firmly pressed into my cheek.

"No. Well… I suppose that's to be expected," Jaques said - unfortunately completely serious. He cleared his throat, toying with a cheese-flavoured biscuit I'd hastily brought out to replace my shortbread selection. "It must be hard… moving to a completely new place and starting over. I don't know if I could do it."

"It wasn't too much of a challenge for me. My mother was French, so I have a bit of an advantage when it comes to the language." Jaques was taking a circuitous approach, but he must be building up a picture of all the potential players in this deadly game of murder.

"And how are you finding it living in Sellenoise? Have you made friends? Is there anyone special in your life right now?"

"Most people here are very friendly," I told him, regrettably unable to say *all*, but everyone needed a little adversity in their life - even if it came courtesy of their neighbours.

Since they'd stopped trying to force me out of the little cul-de-sac, things had certainly been more amiable - but then, almost anything could be considered more amiable than the time I'd blown up my neighbour in retaliation for him dumping waste on my property. "I'm good friends with the local postmistress, and then there's Marius, of course."

"Marius? Ah, the local police agent," Jaques said, a line appearing between his eyebrows for a few moments, before he remembered to whom I was referring… which was concerning, considering that Marius' presence at the scene of the crime should be analysed in the same way I was being analysed right now. "He is your… friend?"

"We work together, but yes, I consider him a friend."

"You're already working for the police, that's good. You used to work for them before, too, didn't you… back in England?" Here, Jaques frowned. "I'm not sure my computer translated things correctly when I was running background checks…"

I knew exactly what he was wondering about, but his computer would have translated it perfectly. I'd once worked for the police under the dubious title of 'psychic' - but that had been something I'd fallen into accidentally, when I'd imagined that the police wouldn't be able to believe that I just had exceptional powers of observation. After things had taken a swift turn South, I'd decided that a fresh start in France was needed - a start that included being honest about my past. "The police believed I was psychic, but in truth, I'm just very good at noticing things."

"I see," Jaques said, meaning the opposite.

I took another sip of my wine as I mulled over why he might have delved so deeply into my past. Jaques Laurent had really done his homework for this case.

"So… have you solved many murders?" he asked, apparently wanting to push this point a little further. I wondered if he was trying to push it so far as to suggest that I had somehow orchestrated the crimes in all of the cases I had later 'solved'. He wouldn't be the first to hold that opinion.

"I assisted with some, yes, but I am a psychotherapist by trade, and that is where I focus most of my time... with the exception of occasionally helping Marius - but that's only because the municipal police are currently understaffed." And by understaffed, I meant they had a staff of exactly one.

"The house is looking good," he said out of the blue with only the slightest of glances at the place where there'd once been a hole in the floor.

"Thank you. It's taking a lot of time and money, but I think I've finally got beyond keeping it from falling down and have progressed to actually making improvements." I looked around the room we were sitting in and was filled with a warm sense of pride at what had been done and the hard work that was evident everywhere I looked. Converting a barn was no simple task. It could be done badly, or done beautifully. I was very hopeful that, in my case, the barn would be going from the former to the latter. With every new element that was added - like the suspended walkway from the mezzanine to the old hayloft, which was well on its way to becoming a second bedroom - I saw more of my vision coming together. Once the ensuite in the master bedroom was complete, things would really be cooking. All it needed was time... and a heck of a lot more money.

I'd been warned that the house was a money pit when I'd won it in a raffle - something which almost all of the locals had considered the opposite of a prize that someone would actually want. I couldn't deny that they had been right about the house seizing fistfuls of cash and chomping them down to nothing, but I now believed that the counter argument to money pits was that money has to be spent on something - so why not use it to forge a forever home? Personally, I thought that decision created far more tangible joy than piling the cash up in a bank for a rainy day.

"I like it. Are you planning to share it with anyone?" Jaques asked, stretching back in his chair, like a panther flexing. He appeared to be completely relaxed and at ease in the enviable way of people who don't worry what others think of them. I caught a hint of the aftershave he was wearing, and there was something about it that made me think of mountains and campfires. For a split second, I wondered what it might feel like to be wrapped in those arms.

Oh dear.

It had definitely been way too long since I'd spent time alone with a man who wasn't Marius or Damien.

"I share it with Spice," I trilled, my cheeks turning pink, as I focused too much on my wayward thoughts. The irrational human fear that the person I was talking to would somehow be able to read them straight from my face overtook me for a second. "But you didn't mean my dog, did you? In which case, it's just little old me out here on my own." *Wonderful.* Now I was talking as if I was a wolf masquerading as an eighty-year-old granny, trying to trick a girl in a red coat to inspect my alarmingly large teeth.

"I'm sure it won't be that way forever," Jaques said, rubbing his finger and thumb together for a moment as he considered.

"Who knows what the future holds?" I said, still stuck in cheery mode. "But back to the murder - is there anything I can help you with?" A sure fire way to know when a conversation wasn't going well was when murder became a more inviting topic. I couldn't even blame the wine, as I'd only taken two sips. Perhaps I should have had more.

"There is, actually," Jaques said with carefully practiced reluctance - as if his next words hadn't been the main reason he'd come here tonight. "It's become apparent that there is a significant language barrier, which is impeding our investigation. With your lack of connection to the victim and most of the other witnesses - combined with your bilingual ability and track record for helping the police - I think you may be useful when it comes to solving this crime and ensuring that justice is done. That's what matters in the end, isn't it?" His tawny eyes zeroed in on mine. "Doing the right thing is what's truly important, and it would be terrible if someone were to get away with murder, simply because something got lost in translation."

I'd observed that Jaques had used psychological techniques earlier in the conversation, but that was nothing compared to this. The way he'd prefaced asking me to join his team by making points that no one with any sort of conscience could disagree with was a classic sales technique. Agreeing with something initially made it far more likely that I would say yes when the big question itself arrived. It was with a jolt that I suddenly wondered if the conversation prior to this new topic had been just another facet designed to get me on his side… by making me feel an emotional connection with him. The worst part was, I knew it had worked. "You want me to help you… as a translator?"

Jaques pulled a thoughtful face - as if I were the one who'd made this sudden leap of logic. "A translator would be useful… someone who understands the minds of the British," he added, narrowing his eyes - as if it was a great cosmic mystery.

"British people are easy. We're either drinking tea, or thinking about the next cup," I joked, back to speaking in that strange jolly voice. It was my way of covering up how silly I felt for thinking that Jaques was interested in more than just solving the case - or in this instance, getting someone to solve it for him.

"I see," Jaques said, unfortunately taking me completely

seriously again and nodding like I'd just told him some great national secret. "I think you can be more than just a translator with your prior experience."

"I already have a job working with the local police," I said, thinking that Jaques had not actually referred to this new role as a job at all - which probably meant I was expected to do it for free, out of the goodness of my heart. While I liked to help people where and when I could, that 'goodness' definitely didn't extend to doing gendarmes' jobs for them, when they weren't trying all that hard to get anything done themselves.

"I don't want you working with some local police loser. I want you to work for me!" Jaques said, his eyes flashing and revealing far more about himself than he might have liked. Jaques Laurent had a temper… and it clearly didn't take much for him to lose it and show his true feelings.

I fixed him with a long, steady look. "I don't have any qualifications as a translator, so I think it would be far more appropriate for you to engage the services of someone who does it as their profession. It's also obvious that you believe there is a big difference in the standard of police work between the municipal force and your own team. I just don't think I would be able to function at your level. It's probably best that I stick with the local police loser."

Jaques pressed his lips into a thin line. "Come on, I didn't really mean…"

"Oh, but you did," I interrupted, before he could get any further with his backtracking. "It's perfectly all right. I appreciate you sharing your true feelings. I wish you luck, both with finding a translator and with solving the case," I finished, standing up and indicating that this strange faux social visit was over.

"Justine, I didn't mean to upset you. It's very important to me that you join my team. I'm sure we can come up with some sort of arrangement to compensate you for your time," Jaques said... far too late. "I need your help with this."

I tilted my head at him. "I think you should focus more of your time and attention on solving the murder and less of it on palming off your duties on someone else." I nearly added 'and insulting her friends' but that could remain unspoken. He knew exactly what he'd done.

"I just need a go between. I can bring you on as a consultant. That's what you do for Marius, isn't it?" he said - magically remembering the local police loser's name, now that he was desperately trying to salvage this situation.

I considered him coldly, unable to stop myself from feeling hurt by everything that had happened this evening and how far I'd let it go. "I don't want to work with you," I told him flatly, indicating that he should be leaving right now.

Jaques shot me a pained look and opened his mouth - undoubtedly to try some new technique that was supposed to win me over - but at that moment, my front door sprung open.

"Cuckoo! I thought I'd pop in to see how you're doing, Justine. I've just heard the terrible details of - oh!" Marissa stopped short when she spotted my company.

Jaques threw me one last look filled with regret and longing, then he sidestepped Marissa and walked out of my house.

My friend watched him go, before looking from me to Jaques and back again. "Who... was that?" she said in an excited whisper, miming fanning her face as she did so. Her sharp eyes moved to the two glasses of wine that were currently sitting on my kitchen table.

"It was just a friend. No, actually - it wasn't a friend or a friendly meeting at all," I said, answering reflexively before correcting myself, knowing she'd be drawing all of the wrong conclusions.

"Shame… I wouldn't mind a friendly meeting with him. What crime would I need to commit to get his attention?" She glanced over and saw my raised eyebrow. "Oh, come on. It's not hard to work out what he does for a living. He may not be in uniform, but he's still in uniform, if you know what I mean."

"I thought the same thing," I agreed, and then inclined my head towards the half-full bottle of wine that was still on the table.

"Go on then," she said, sitting where Jaques had previously been while I got her a fresh glass. "I don't suppose he was here to arrest you for murdering that poor woman? The press release I found in the *Guéret Globe* did all it could to gloss over the gory details, but you can't really gloss over someone being hit by a giant axe thing, can you? It must have been awful to see…"

"You know I can't say more about that," I told her, well aware that she was hoping I might be persuaded to fill in some of the gory details that the paper, which she'd gone out of her way to find, had glossed over.

"Then say something more about that handsome man who just left. For example, why didn't you tie him to the chair?"

I shook my head, but I couldn't stop the smile from jumping onto my lips. For all of his faults, which were apparently many, Jaques was certainly not unattractive. "I know he's probably the only potentially eligible man of a similar age to me within twenty miles, but I think I can afford to be a bit more choosy. A pretty face does not guarantee a good man."

"Not the only eligible man," Marissa countered, shooting me a curious look, which turned into an eye roll when I didn't take the bait. "Still, that does bring me to the real reason I came here tonight, which was not to fish around for more details about the murder, I promise. Well, it was half that, but you're no fun and clearly haven't had enough wine to drink…" She pushed my glass closer to me. "In the meantime, I wanted to get your name down for the annual Sellenoise Singles Celebration Day this Friday."

"The… what?" I asked, hoping I'd somehow misunderstood what sounded like an event that would pretend to celebrate single people, whilst fostering the not so secret agenda of forcing them to couple up.

"It's a fun dancing and talking event that we hold in the square. If you're single, you get to wear a special sign. That's how you can spot all of the other single people!"

"And then do what… hunt them down?" I commented, thinking that this was everything I'd thought it would be and worse, if it came with easy identification for the benefit of spectators.

"You could do! But not with a weapon… with your charm," Marissa added when she saw my expression. "Come on, Justine, I need you there. I don't know if you've noticed, but this town is hardly bursting with singletons, and it's a local tradition! Everyone knows you're here on your own, so you can't skip it. Otherwise, everyone will think that…"

"…that I'm staying home, drowning my sorrows in a tub of ice-cream and a bottle of wine?" I suggested, wondering whether to tell Marissa that her argument was going about as well as Jaques'. Perhaps the pair could meet up for productive discussions on how to be less rubbish at persuading people to do what they wanted.

Marissa smiled brightly at me.

I glared back. "What about you? Will you be wearing a signifier of solitude?" I asked, knowing that Marissa was also single.

"Goodness, no. As the event organiser, I couldn't possibly…" She saw my look and hastily changed tack. "Everyone knows I'm not interested in saddling myself with a man. I enjoy my own company. The idea of someone coming in and taking up half of my space and just being there all the time makes me feel positively unwell."

"Why do you think you feel that way?" I asked.

Marissa clapped her hands together in front of her face. "No! No therapy. I'm allowed to have made a decision that goes against the mainstream just because I want to. It's final, and I'm happy… which is what matters, isn't it?"

I nodded my head, unable to find a fault with that. Even if there was a reason that could be unravelled behind someone's decision to do something, if the end result was their happiness, there was no real benefit to unpacking the past and getting to the bottom of it. "Why can't I be the same as you? I'm happy here. I'm happier than I've ever been," I said, suddenly feeling all warm and fuzzy when I realised the truth of my own words.

"Because, my dear Justine, I know you could be happier still. That's why you're doing this event. And also because I need to get the numbers up."

"If you think I'm going to fall for a seventy-year-old, who glows in the dark from background radiation build up caused by not airing his cellar every year, then you are sorely mistaken."

"You won't be set up with anyone, I promise."

"Just offered up, like a sacrifice to heathen gods?" I suggested.

Marissa pulled a face that implied she thought I was being silly and overreacting when I was convinced that, if anything, I was probably being far too reasonable. Anything that made her think I was up for this event would fall under that category. "You'll love it. I'll come and get you on the day."

"Marissa, I don't want…"

"Must dash! Goodbye until then. Ta-ta!"

"Marissa, I'm not…"

But the postmistress was already back at the front door, waggling her fingers and beaming like I'd promised to hand over my winning lottery ticket. "It's going to be brilliant fun!"

"Marissa!" I tried one last time.

"Super-duper fun!" and with that, she shut the door behind her and vanished.

7

THE MEMORY OF CRIME

It was several days before I thought about the murder again.
Well, almost. I had the kind of mind that was never willing to let sleeping unsolved murders lie, so it was constantly being chewed over somewhere in the back of my brain, but I did keep my nose out of it.

After my strange meeting with Jaques, he hadn't contacted me and I certainly hadn't reached out to him. I had no desire to be the gendarme's snitch, just so that his life could be a little more convenient. It had been the cause of many loud sighs and tuts to myself when I'd been alone in the house. I'd wondered whether my decision was unreasonable, considering that, in the past, Marius and I had done most of the work for the gendarmes anyway, because they hadn't been interested. And yet, somehow, this felt even more outrageous, although I couldn't put a finger on why that was.

My resolve to not get involved was further shaken when Alex turned up at my door. I silently despaired at Damien's willingness to 'help my business' and invited him in, unsurprised to hear that he wanted to discuss therapy to help him process what had happened to Fern. It was one of those times when I'd briefly wished I lived closer to a large city, just so I could refer them all to a different therapist, who didn't have conflicts of interest.

"Would you like to come through to the sitting room? I can get you a cup of tea or coffee and we can have a chat," I said, knowing that was the most I could offer.

Alex scuffed his feet on the doorstep. "No, actually. When I said therapy, I suppose what I really meant is support. I don't have too many friends, beyond my work colleagues, and this isn't something I want to bring them in on."

I could understand that. Nothing said 'no promotions forever' quite like being a possible suspect in the murder of your fiancée. And as her partner, Alex was unfortunately, statistically speaking, the most likely to have murdered Fern.

A fact I reminded myself of when he said the next thing.

"I just need help sorting out the apartment. The gendarmes have been through everything and taken whatever they wanted to take. They told me I could go back there now, but I can't - not with all of her things just lying around, reminding me of her, everywhere I look." He took a deep shuddering breath. "I know it hasn't hit me yet. Not really. Right now, I feel like I'm falling through the air without knowing when the ground is going to rise up and hit me."

I nodded understandingly, well aware that grief came in many forms and affected everyone differently. The person responsible for Fern's death would probably also be experiencing an absence of the expected reaction - much like Alex - but they would undoubtedly be taking pains to conceal it... like Alex had just done. While it would be foolish to not have some serious reservations, I still wanted to help if I could. "What do you mean by sorting out the apartment?" I asked, wary of signing up for hard labour, when I had more than enough of it to do at home.

"Can you just come with me? I need company… someone to be there."

A person with a better sense of self-preservation would not have found themselves pulling up outside of the beige rendered building in Guéret half an hour later. I kissed goodbye to the slow morning of working on the house I'd planned in my head. To my credit, I'd driven my own car over to Alex and Fern's place on the grounds of it being more convenient for him not to have to drop me back - but truly, I wasn't about to get in a car alone with any of the other witnesses. Not when one of them was good enough at advanced planning to design a boobytrap capable of killing someone. Of course… going into what could be the killer's lair was also not the brightest move, but you couldn't win every battle.

"I don't want to stay here," Alex announced when we were in the corridor outside of the door that led to the apartment. The floor was covered with ancient brown tiles, and the frame that ran around the door was yellowed with age - apart from at one place at the top, where the paint had been rubbed off. "I'm just grabbing some of my stuff. I'm going to stay with someone from work, who said I could crash on his sofa until I figure everything out. I reckon I might go back to the UK. This all used to feel like an adventure - especially after meeting Fern out here - but now it feels like the adventure is over. I was headhunted during a company expansion, and it was an interesting opportunity, but now…"

"I always think it's a good idea to give big decisions a couple of weeks to settle," I said, knowing that rushing into things due to a negative incident didn't always result in a positive outcome.

"I'll think on it," Alex promised, sighing when he opened

the door and revealed a place in total disarray. "That stuck up gendarme said they'd been in and gathered evidence, but he failed to mention they'd trashed the place. It's going to take me forever to sort this out. I'll do it another day. I can't face it now."

I followed him inside to the magnolia main room, where cream sofas hinted of no pets or children, and various ornaments sat around, looking a lot like they'd been ordered from a magazine just for the sake of ambience. Standing in this room, I could have been in London, not the heart of France. The place had looked messy when we'd walked in, but now that I was closer, I realised it was only because of a few scattered magazines and tossed cushions that would take two minutes to pick up.

"Make yourself at home, if you can," Alex called from somewhere deeper in the apartment.

I walked around the room with my hands in my pockets, wondering whether I should be trying to spot clues when the gendarmes had already been in and would have surely taken away anything that they'd deemed relevant... and I was definitely, totally not getting involved.

The kitchen was opposite the open plan lounge area. When I walked over, I noticed there was a neat nook that might have once been a built in cupboard. It had since been converted into an area for a desk. A devil's ivy draped down from its place on a shelf of true crime novels and thrillers, and there were various files with weekly dates written on them that were neatly stacked next to the computer that had been left behind by the gendarmes - presumably after they'd cloned the hard drive, if they'd been doing their jobs properly.

I glanced around and nudged the mouse, amused when a picture of Sherlock Holmes flashed up as the screensaver. It was obvious that Fern had been a bit of a crime buff. My steps carried me further into the kitchen and I saw the signs of daily life that had been so suddenly interrupted. The fridge was covered in magnets featuring photos of Alex and Fern on holiday somewhere warm, and then skiing in the winter. A card with a dentist's name on it was pinned beneath a smiley face, never to be contacted by Fern again, and a half-written shopping list served as a reminder that a life had been interrupted.

"How did you and Fern meet?" I called out to Alex as I moved on to the kitchen. The gendarmes had given up by the time they'd got here, because nothing seemed disturbed. It was that, or perhaps they imagined people didn't hide secrets in the kitchen.

"Lyra brought me along to one of Damien's get-togethers, and Fern came with Miranda. She was in Creuse to write an article. Miranda had got her a meeting with a fashion designer, who was hiding out down here after receiving death threats in the wake of a controversial show and wanted to draw attention to his plight. Fern was great at writing about crime, but it wasn't without its risks."

"Did she decide to move to Creuse after meeting you?" I asked, wondering if romance had been the catalyst.

"It's a bit more complicated than that," Alex said, reappearing carrying a black holdall. His face was pale, and I got the impression that what he'd said about Fern's death not hitting him yet might be on the cusp of changing. "I'd like to think I was a big part of her reasons for staying, but I think she was primarily inspired by the fashion designer in hiding. If it was a good enough place for him to run to and feel safe, it was good enough for her. She found it hard to discuss her past, even with me. At some point, not too long ago, she was involved in a terrible incident where she was badly burned and had to have surgery. She would never put her hair up, because there were still patches missing where her skin was scarred, even after the surgery. Fern was just like the rest of us. No matter what we might tell ourselves and each other, we're all trying to get away from something, aren't we?" Alex tilted his head at me, his eyes suddenly going all serious.

I answered him with a small smile, not dwelling on my own situation for too long. I'd already made my peace with it. "New starts can be many things for many different people. I suppose it would depend on your definition of 'getting away from something'. Did you have something to get away from when you decided to take the job here?" I asked, curious about Alex's own story.

"We've all got our secrets," he said, going all mysterious.

"Oh?" I prompted as mildly as I could, secretly hoping that this would be over soon. The longer I spent here, finding questions falling from my lips, the more I felt myself being sucked into this mystery, like sand through a timer. I was approaching the point of no return.

Alex sighed, before apparently deciding that he could be persuaded to talk about it after all. "Well, in my case…" He stopped talking and frowned at me when we both heard the click of someone interfering with the front door.

"Did you lock it?" I asked him, immediately on edge.

"It locks on the outside when you close it," he whispered, staring down the slim corridor towards the front door with a look of frozen terror on his face.

"Hide," I decided, sensing that Alex certainly hadn't expected us to have company during this morning's mission.

A few moments later, we were squashed against the wall in the gap behind the sofa - that had needed to be enlarged significantly. I pulled the blanket that had been neatly folded on the back of the sofa over us, hopefully covering anything that was sticking out, but in terms of an effective hiding place, I couldn't help feeling it was probably about as brilliant as a child standing behind a curtain with their feet sticking out. Our only hope was that the person trying to get into the apartment wasn't expecting anyone to be inside.

"You'll keep me safe, right?" Alex whispered, apparently deciding that therapists were the same thing as bodyguards.

The door clicked open.

Footsteps approached down the corridor.

8

THE KEEPER OF KEYS

Alex gripped my arm, like a mother gripping the door handle when her teenager is driving, as the footsteps came closer. Beneath the blanket, where things were already getting pretty hot and sweaty, I frowned, mentally calculating just how long it had taken for the intruder to get the door open. I was pretty sure the answer was not long at all. That meant they were either a professional burglar, who opened doors to make their very illegal living, or… they'd had a key. I thought I knew which one was more likely - especially when I noted that the footsteps were pronounced, suggesting that the intruder was wearing high heels. Last time I checked, stilettos weren't standard thief attire outside of Hollywood.

"Where is it?" a female voice muttered in English.

"Looking for something?" I said, throwing the blanket off with a flourish and standing up in an impressive sweep - or what would have been an impressive sweep, if I'd managed to do it without having to prise myself out from between the sofa and wall, like a particularly stubborn champagne cork.

Ursula looked at me with an expression of mild surprise.

"Why were you behind the sofa?" she asked, as if it was *my* presence here which was questionable. Alex popped up behind me and Ursula's eyebrows shot up.

"We heard an intruder entering the property and took precautions," I explained coolly, not allowing this woman - who was very used to getting her own way - to get off the hook.

"Why are you in my apartment?" Alex exploded.

"I have a key," Ursula said, waving something that did indeed look like a key.

"No you don't!" Alex argued.

"Well, technically, I shouldn't have a key, but I kept it from when I lived here. Didn't Fern tell you that this used to be my place? Derek and I stayed for a while whilst we were house hunting, and I recommended it to Fern when she arrived here, before you got together. I may have kept a copy of the key when I returned everything to the landlord."

"Why would you want to enter the apartment without permission?" I asked, unimpressed with her explanation so far.

Ursula didn't even blush. "I didn't want to bother you with something so trivial. I thought you'd be at work, Alex, but I suppose what happened was very upsetting. Of course you should take some time off for yourself. I should have called you."

"What's your reason for entering the apartment?" I repeated, sensing that Alex was close to losing his cool and forcefully kicking Ursula out of the home he'd shared with Fern. Something told me she might be missing from his Christmas card list this year. Ursula would be missing from everyone's list, if she was the one who'd killed Fern.

"Oh, it's nothing really. I just lent her something and I want it back. See? It sounds silly now, when she's, you know…"

"Dead?" I finished for her.

Ursula did the hand waving thing she loved to do when she didn't consider something to be particularly important. "It makes it rather awkward, doesn't it? I mean, what kind of person would I be, if the first thing I did after Fern died was to ask if I could have my hair clip back? I thought it would be better to be subtle about it."

There was a pause while all three of us considered the current situation and how it did not in any way, shape, or form fit the definition of 'subtle'.

"There it is! I'll just get it and be on my way," she said, making a dive for the coffee table. Unfortunately for Ursula, I was much closer and scooped the clip up easily, glancing down at the tortoiseshell clasp with its designer brand embossed in silver. "Do you have any proof that this is yours?"

Ursula threw her head back and huffed. "No, I didn't come armed with a receipt, like some crazy coupon lady. Look, it's been years since I got it, but it's important to me, and I only loaned it to Fern when she wanted her hair off her face when we were out with Miranda last week. She never tied her hair back, but the wind was annoying her when we were sitting outside. I know how complicated things like this can get when someone dies and those close to them aren't aware of the provenance of every single item they owned. I'm sure I can dig out some photos, if you really insist. In any case, you know I'm taking it, so if you believe I'm stealing, then the onus is on you to provide proof of that, isn't it? Good. Thanks," she said, snatching it from me.

I allowed her to take it, having inspected it for long enough. "I don't think that's correct," I told her mildly, but her eyes immediately flashed with the challenge.

"Tell your friend the gendarme about it. See if I care! I

don't have time for this." She spun on a very pointy heel and stalked back towards the door.

"Ursula!" Alex called in such a surprisingly assertive way that she was forced to stop and turn to see what he wanted. "Key," he said, holding out his hand.

"I was only keeping it as a souvenir from my time here," Ursula said, handing it over sulkily. There was something about her expression when the key fell into Alex's waiting hand that made me think she might not have completely finished using it.

"I should report you to the gendarmes for this," Alex said, showing that all was not fuzzy friendships in the group.

"I'm busy this Friday. I'll see you on Friday for our session," Ursula said to me, as if the past five minutes hadn't happened.

"You're giving her therapy?" Alex asked when she'd gone, slamming the door pointedly behind her. I supposed I should be pleased that he hadn't assumed we were meeting up for a fun coffee between friends.

"I am not," I told him emphatically, hoping that at least one of Damien's guests would listen to me when I said 'no'.

"You don't mind me talking to you though, do you? I just mean informally, like we're doing right now. I wouldn't ask, but I don't really have anyone else. It was just me and…" He choked up for a moment and took a shuddering breath.

"You have to understand that I can't offer you confidentiality," I said, feeling sorry for the man I was talking to, in spite of my stance on providing therapy.

"Yes, of course… I see," Alex said, looking frazzled by the situation he found himself in.

"Are you going to call the gendarmes and tell them about Ursula? I think you probably should," I said, hoping to poke Alex into doing something I really didn't want to do myself, because I was too annoyed with Jaques to risk speaking to him again. "Every single detail, no matter how small, might hold the answer to who's behind what was done to Fern," I added, sounding like the police spokesperson at a press conference. It was a cliché, but I knew from firsthand experience that it was also true - because I was often the one who noticed the small details that added up to a bigger, uglier picture.

"They might not believe me. That head honcho gendarme has been applying pressure in every way he can think of to get me to confess. He even went to my work and asked my boss about what sort of person I am, and if I've ever shown any violent tendencies, or built mechanical contraptions - which was a ridiculous thing to ask, given my job." His expression darkened.

"You said your job involves troubleshooting and safety, didn't you? And you work with Lyra?"

Alex sighed and looked tired. "At the same company, yes, but not together. She works designing the kind of mechanical contraption that the gendarmes should actually be interested in. I'm just responsible for health and safety. I work out if stuff is going to break, and if it could be considered dangerous. It hardly fits the bill, does it?"

I nodded vaguely as I considered what he'd said... and how he'd strongly implied that Lyra did fit the bill, whether he'd intended to or not. "Do you know if Lyra was excluded from any get-togethers of the other women in the expat group?" I asked, remembering Lyra's reaction when the 'gossip group' had been mentioned by Derek.

Alex scuffed a foot on the floor, his eyes not meeting mine. "It's a bit awkward. When Lyra brought me along to meet Damien and the others, I think she was hoping that it might spark something between us, but instead, I met Fern. I suppose there's a chance that Lyra regrets making the introduction now." He shot me a quick look. "But not that much! I mean... there's no way, right?"

"You should probably also mention that to the gendarmes when you call them," I said, not wanting to encourage any finger pointing without any evidence to support it, but also not underestimating what people will do for love... or perhaps more accurately, for jealousy. "I'll back up your statement if it's needed, but I do think it would be better coming from you. It will show that you're trying to help solve the case, which will go in your favour." The further away I could stay from Jaques, the better.

"I suppose you're right. I'll do it," he promised.

"Thank you," I replied, relieved that it was off my plate and required no further involvement from me, but I couldn't shake the feeling that - like it or not - I'd become a part of this the day I'd said yes to the surprise party invitation.

Damien's little friendship group had fractured, and now the broken shards were trying to cut each other down to size. The question was, who had taken a hammer to the tightly knit Brits?

Or in this case... a halberd.

* * *

The light was flashing on my answering machine when I returned from the morning's trip to witness an attempted burglary. I popped the kettle on and pressed play.

"I suppose you're out doing something for your new employer right now. I had to twist your arm to get you to agree to help me out occasionally, and now you're working with *him*? He'll do anything to avoid actually doing his job. What did he do, appeal to your ego? Wine and dine you? I'm just... disappointed. Bye." Marius' final word faded into the ether. The message finished and the computerised voice asked me if I wanted to delete the message, or return the call.

"Oh, for goodness' sake!" I said with such frustration that Spice whined and shot me an uncertain look.

I ruffled his soft ears to show that he had nothing to worry about, whilst silently plotting the imminent and messy demise of Jaques Laurent. Apparently, it hadn't been enough for him to come to my house and try to play mind games. Now, he was also reaching into other areas of my life and making trouble for me there. "Marius is right about one thing - he really will try anything to avoid doing his actual job," I said out loud, thinking that, if Jaques could focus as much of his attention on this investigation as he was lavishing on ruining my life, the case would be solved in no time at all.

"As if I didn't already have enough to deal with!" I muttered, resigning myself to losing the afternoon, too. Words like that couldn't be left lying between me and Marius. I decided I was going to work with the police after all… just not the gendarmes.

9

SECOND GUESSING

Both of Sellenoise's bars had their tables and chairs scattered at regular intervals throughout the town square. Even though *La Petite Grenouille* was often avoided by the locals, due to the proprietor's eccentric behaviour - which included impromptu opera singing - his food and drink had won people over today. Or perhaps it was the good weather that had tempted them, because even his tables were filled with people drinking up the sunshine. Creuse was a green and pleasant land, which told you an awful lot about the amount of rain that fell, but the summers were still a great deal nicer than those I remembered in England, and the French sunshine always evoked memories of my mother whenever a truly beautiful day smiled down upon the countryside.

I nodded to the mayor, who was sipping something alcoholic at the town's other bar, where he so often held court. The door of the municipal police station looked bright and cheerful in the August sunshine. I'd been brought in by Marius to help sort out his filing system, in order to facilitate the solving of future crimes and avoid anything being lost or overlooked - due to the total disarray that everything had been kept in. During that time, I'd also grown tired of the flaking paint on the front door that made the entire station look tatty. *First impressions are important,* I'd told Marius when I'd stripped it back to the natural wood and repainted it in a shade that said 'police' to me.

What looked a lot less bright and sunny was the gendarme car parked outside of the station, informing me that the trouble starter responsible for the unusual answer machine message was apparently still here, stirring the pot. If I'd been wearing long sleeves, I would have rolled them up. Instead, I gritted my teeth and prepared to do battle.

I strode down the corridor with its slightly sticky linoleum floor, ready to bump into my new adversary at any second. All I found when I turned into Marius' office was the local chief of police himself, sitting behind his desk with a bleak expression on his face as he stared at a blank wall.

"A painting would brighten up that space," I said, walking in and noting that there was no sign of Jaques Laurent lurking in any of the corners.

"Your new best friend has just gone out," Marius replied, looking gloomier still. "He came here claiming that he was looking for you, but I think he just visited to rub your new job in my face and tell me that you won't be working with me any more."

"And you believed him?" I said, arching a single eyebrow and waiting for Marius to look at me.

"Why wouldn't I? He's a gendarme, and his job is solving serious crimes, while I chase after lost dogs. He didn't hesitate to remind me of that. You've worked with the police in England in the past, so it makes sense that once he'd figured that out, he scooped you up. There's nothing I can do about it. I'm merely a municipal chief of police at a police station with no other police agents. I suppose I'm just surprised. I thought you didn't want to have a more involved role in policing, otherwise I'd have asked you to work with me as an agent."

"I did say that, and I'm not working with Jaques," I told him more plainly.

Marius' forehead furrowed as he finally processed what I was telling him. "Then why did that smug peacock tell me you're his new consultant?"

I glanced back in the direction of the entrance, before sidestepping the question. "Where did he go? There's a car out front."

"After I phoned you, he said he was going to look around town, or something. I assumed he had a meeting with you about some new information he claimed to have found out this morning - information that he deliberately waved in front of my face without telling me what it was, because it's not my job to know anything about the case. It's frankly ridiculous when I was the one who was there when the crime actually occurred. I could even be a suspect!" he finished with an exasperated hand flourish.

"You should have told him that," I said with my tongue pressed into my cheek.

"We don't all have the ear of the overlord," he replied, not looking impressed by my attempt at humour. "I suppose you're in the know, now that you're in cahoots with the gendarmes?"

"I do know, actually… but not because I'm working with Monsieur Laurent. He paid me a visit a few nights ago and did everything he could to persuade me to work with him, but I refused. Anything he told you to the contrary is incorrect, and he won't be persuading me to change my mind any time soon."

Marius tilted his head and looked alarmingly curious. "He did everything he could?"

"The point is, I said no... so you can stop being grumpy with me."

"Grumpy?!" Marius exploded, standing up and looking the very definition of the word. He sat down a second later when he probably realised exactly that. "Sorry. You're right, I shouldn't have taken him at his word. Now that I think about it, everything he did during our brief meeting was supposed to make me resent you. Perhaps he's trying to divide us, so that you'll go to him in order to get back at me."

"That's very perceptive of you," I said, before Marius rightly shot me a glare for being patronising. "That information he was brandishing is nothing terribly useful, I'm afraid. I went with Alex to the place where he lived with Fern. While he was packing his things, Ursula broke in using a spare key she'd kept from a time when she and Derek had lived in the same apartment. She claimed she was there to pick up a hair clip that she'd lent to Fern prior to her death. According to her, she thought breaking in would be the most convenient solution." I raised my eyebrows.

"That's a rubbish excuse," Marius said, mirroring my own thoughts.

"I'm not completely convinced that the hair clip was what Ursula was really there to get. It's probably worth thinking on. Not that either of us should be thinking about any of this," I hastily added.

"Very true," Marius agreed.

We lasted a whole five seconds.

"What motive could Ursula have had for wanting Fern to be dead and buried... and why build such a complicated trap to do it?" he mused, looking equal parts horrified and fascinated.

"I'm not sure," I confessed. "I feel like we know so little, and yet, the pieces of the puzzle must all be here somewhere, just waiting for someone to find them and put them together. But not us."

"What if…? No, it would be a bad idea," Marius said, shaking his head and pretending to change his mind halfway through the sentence.

"We both know it's not our job to get involved. Is it worth the risk? Not to mention the fact that Jaques will get all the credit if we do find out what happened," I added with a sigh. "Maybe I should have said yes to working with him and taken payment and glory over slogging away with no hope of reward."

Marius shot me such a disgusted look that I burst out laughing. "Oh, come on. I'm kidding. Who doesn't love slogging away for no reward?"

"You have a very strange sense of humour," he told me, looking surly. A shadow flickered across the office window when an errant breeze blew a leafy branch in front of the sunlight - reminding me that time was passing, and with it, plans came closer to reaching their fruition.

Like the plans of a particular gendarme.

"How long did Jaques say he would be gone for?" I asked, thinking about the car parked outside of the police station.

"He didn't say, because I'm too beneath him to know any of the details of his fascinating life," Marius said with a huge eye roll.

"We shouldn't be here when he gets back, which will probably be momentarily," I said, having formed an insight into the gendarme's own inner workings and his use of psychology on other people.

Marius followed me out into the corridor. We were about to walk towards the entrance when we heard the sound of talking, and the unmistakeable voice of Jaques Laurent rose in laughter, as he approached the exterior door with one of his colleagues. The police station was an old building, a relic from a time before fire escapes were deemed necessary, or prudent. The belief had been that the windows were big enough for people to escape from in the event of a disaster, so why worry? Unfortunately, that meant our only way out was blocked.

We returned to the office and Marius shut the door, dashing over to his window and sliding it open.

"I wish this was both the first and last time that I have to use a window to gain access to, or from, this building," I complained, awkwardly trying to fold myself in half to sideways roll through the window. It was large, but not large enough for that. Panicked by the sound of the gendarmes getting closer, Marius gave me a hefty shove, and I fell headfirst towards the moss and dirt on the ground outside of the window. By some small miracle, my hands hit the floor before my face, and I managed a sort of forward roll somersault that my body warned me I should never attempt again.

"Sorry, we didn't have time," Marius said, landing neatly on his feet next to me. "It looked cool though," he added, apparently thinking 'looking cool' was the compliment I'd been longing for. He turned and slid the window shut as silently as he could, before grabbing my hand and helping me to my feet. Together, we crept around the side of the building and arrived by the same bushes I'd been forced to escape through the last time I'd been trying to avoid someone.

"Not again," I muttered, remembering how little I'd enjoyed that cross-country hike.

"We can just wait," Marius suggested, not so keen to take action now that he was the one facing a cross-country trek through multiple hedgerows.

"Or… we could get across the town square and blend in at one of the bars. Jaques has come back because he knows you'll have contacted me and started an argument. He's hoping that I'll have come here to correct you on his lie, and he'll find us in the middle of a disagreement that he'll then be able to exploit to convince me to work with him. Luckily for us, we know exactly what he's up to. Sitting down and having a civil coffee together will completely throw him."

Staying low, we went back around the building again, before breaking cover and darting across the square - like children playing granny's footsteps.

"Now what?" Marius said when we arrived at a cafe.

I waved at the proprietor, Julian, indicating that we would like two coffees. "Now, we talk about how getting involved with this case is a truly terrible idea. It could land us in a lot of trouble and comes served with an extra helping of danger - given what this killer is capable of. Then, we decide we're going to do it anyway, because not only is Jaques Laurent trying to play us off against each other, he also hasn't made any actual progress with the case. Which one is the bigger sin is up for debate," I finished, not entirely serious about the last bit. "No matter what happens, we should stay out of his way," I added, fixing Marius with a serious look. "We're not looking for trouble - just for justice."

"And we certainly can't have any fun doing it," Marius replied sarcastically, rolling his eyes. He went silent in the sudden sort of way that happens when the person you've been talking about is standing right behind you.

10

THREE'S A CROWD

"There you are, Marius, and Justine is here, too! How nice. Mind if I join you?" Jaques said, spinning a chair in his hand and plonking it down with the back facing us, sitting on it so that his legs were akimbo and his elbows could rest on the back of the chair.

I glanced at Marius, knowing we were both wishing we could answer that question with a negative. "What brings you to Sellenoise, Jaques?" I asked, knowing that two could play at pretending innocence.

"Nothing of great importance. I was checking a few things with Marius. He may be the local chief of police, but that doesn't put him above suspicion!" he said, but followed it with a very obvious wink that would have been enough to get him fired, had anyone who mattered witnessed it. "What were you both chatting about? Has Justine come up with a new concept to revolutionise your filing system?"

"Oh, nothing like that," I said, smiling brightly at him. "We may work together, but first and foremost, Marius and I are very good friends. We never let work come between our friendship!" *Or anyone else,* I thought.

"It's nice that you have time to have coffee. My plate is seriously full," Jaques said, with a long look at me that heavily hinted it was all my fault.

"We wish you all the best with solving the murder. It's a shame that neither of us is qualified to help you," I replied, wondering if I should be enjoying this encounter as much as I was. One thing was for sure, when I looked into Jaques' eyes now, there was a lot less contrived attraction and a lot more murder contained in their depths.

"You're both witnesses, so I'm sure you'll be plenty of help. You were with Alex Hake today, weren't you, Justine?"

"I was. He needed someone to come with him for emotional support when he went to get some things from the apartment he shared with Fern. I was happy to do it, as a favour to someone going through a hard time."

"He called me and said that you were interrupted by Ursula Cooper breaking in. Is that correct?" Jaques asked.

"It is," I said, pleased that the man was capable of doing some police work after all.

"What did you make of that?"

"Probably nothing more than Alex has told you," I said, briefly repeating what Ursula had claimed.

"You didn't... have any insights when you were there?" Jaques pressed.

I should probably take back my previous thought about him doing some actual police work. He was aspiring to be the master of forced delegation. "No blinding flashes of inspiration," I told him with a wan smile. "I assume you'll be speaking to Ursula? I know she shared her reasons for being in the apartment when she was caught, but it is a rather suspicious thing for someone to do after there's been a murder, isn't it? Perhaps she was there to remove some evidence against her. She left with a hair clip. If I were you,

I'd be asking her more questions about why it was so important."

"Of course I'm going to do that," Jaques said, frowning like the suggestion was offensive to him, because it implied I thought he didn't know how to do his own job.

"Excellent. I'll be interested to know what you find out," I said, all smiles - as if I hadn't noticed that I'd said anything wrong.

"It *will* be interesting, but I won't be able to divulge any information. You have made it quite clear that you do not want to aid me in this investigation," Jaques replied, bristling.

"Have I? That's good to know." My smile became a little sharper. "Good luck with the case. Maybe this is the big break!"

Jaques stood up, his forehead furrowing. Uncertainty was written on his face, as he tried to figure out if I was insulting him. "It probably is. Everything cracks under enough pressure. Enjoy your filing and your petty crime," he said with a smirk, turning and striding back across the square with the sort of stiffness that only ever accompanies men who worship the uniform they wear.

"Why did you help him?" Marius asked, frowning at me once the gendarme was gone.

"I didn't," I said with a thin smile. "Ursula did take a hair clip away with her, but I'm all but certain it wasn't what she'd actually come to collect."

"What are we going to do?" Marius asked.

I pulled a thoughtful face.

"You're not thinking of breaking into the apartment, are you? I'm not doing anything illegal!" Marius protested.

"No, you usually get *me* to do it for you instead," I commented dryly.

* * *

For all of his talk about breaking the law, Marius didn't actually put up that much of a fight. I pulled up on the same street that I'd driven to this morning, returning as the burglar, instead of the invited.

"What's the plan? Have you got a lock picking kit? I hear they sell those on the internet, which is why it's a good thing the internet is so unreliable around here. Imagine what would happen if that sort of stuff was readily available! The town would become the Wild West in no time at all," Marius said - as if all it took was consistent deliveries from *Amazon* to achieve the total breakdown of society.

"I think most people wouldn't immediately rush out and buy tools to commit crime, if internet shopping became more common around here," I countered. "They'd probably pick other items first."

"Like bomb making supplies?" he suggested.

I frowned. "Are you basing this on Damien?" I asked, drawing the parallels.

"He gets his weapons from the internet. He told me that he paid a lot for satellite internet and that's what he does with it - he buys weapons. Imagine if that sort of thing spread to the whole town!"

"I think that's just Damien," I said, amused by Marius' assumptions. "In answer to your first question, I don't have a lock picking kit. I do, however, know where the spare key is kept." Living in a fairly remote region populated by people with an average age of seventy - and with a normally low crime rate - meant that keys to doors where not often kept in the most secure of places - and that was when the doors were locked at all. Alex had mentioned that the door to his apartment locked automatically when it was shut, but I'd noticed that the frame which ran around the door had a patch of paint that had worn out from all of the times when the people who lived there had forgotten their keys and reached up to take the spare from the ledge. Ursula had brought her own key to break in, but we would be using the one that had always been there.

But even the best laid plans do not always go to plan, I observed when we approached the door and discovered we weren't alone.

"Lyra! What are you doing here?" I asked when I saw the curly-haired woman hovering outside of the apartment door, staring wistfully at the painted wood. Asking that question not only made it sound like I was supposed to be here, and that she was the unexpected presence, it also meant I'd bought myself some time to think up a good excuse.

"Justine! I feel so silly now. I only came because I thought Alex would be at work and no one would be around. I know it's ridiculous, but I just wanted to be somewhere that felt close to her. I don't have another way, and I'm not sure when they're going to get round to the funeral, what with all of the..." She waved a wobbly hand, meaning the ongoing murder investigation.

"You were close to Fern?" I asked with some surprise, remembering what Alex had said about Lyra's feelings for him, and the way that Fern, Miranda, and Ursula had been as thick as thieves - while Lyra was left out in the cold.

"Yes, we had lots in common. We both loved a good crime thriller, so we sort of had a book club for just the two of us. True crime was also a shared passion. I'm a documentary fan and Fern was into podcasts. She listened every week and was completely engrossed. I think she had a very high level subscription to her favourite podcast - *Cold Case Crackers* - the type where you pay money and get early access and can contribute and so on. They're certainly going to miss her now she's gone. It was nice having a friend here. It's hard to meet other people when you're not completely fluent in the lingo, but I am working on it."

"Good for you," I said, feeling sympathetic. There was a big difference between people who moved and tried, and those who stubbornly refused to speak a single word of the language of the country they'd chosen to move to.

Lyra nodded. "It might sound strange, but we actually bonded over our shared attraction to Alex, although - that was something one of us had to put behind us," she said with a slight smile. "He's a good man. Fern was lucky to have him."

"And he, her?" I asked, curious about how over her feelings Lyra truly was.

"No relationship is ever perfect," she said with a shrug. "In any case, it didn't come between us at all. I suppose I always feel a bit left out, being the only one in the group without someone else. Fern would go out with Miranda and Ursula to gossip about their husbands and partners, which wasn't my scene at all. But now you're here! So, that's good, isn't it? Alex is also technically single again, but… that's different," she said, suddenly looking grave. "I am going to miss her a great deal. No more film nights, and no more talking about the books we like. It's such a dreadful waste when someone does something so terrible to someone else." Her forehead furrowed.

"Would you like to go inside? Marius and I are here to investigate a small security breach that took place earlier in the day," I said, managing to make it sound official and reasonable - helped by the fact that Marius was dressed in his uniform. I was also relying on Lyra not thinking too carefully about anything right now. It was not very ethical to take advantage of the situation, but Marius and I needed every advantage we could get, if we wanted this case to be a distant memory. Otherwise, we could be saddled with Jaques and his manipulations for the foreseeable future.

"How kind of you both!" Lyra said, making me feel even worse. I wondered what would happen when she mentioned this to Alex, but decided I'd just stick with the excuse I'd made up and hope that he got on board with it. It was a gamble, but one that needed to be taken. If Ursula was serious about whatever it was that she'd been here to steal this morning, then she would undoubtedly try to get in again when her interview with the useful idiot Jaques Laurent was finished. With Alex unwilling to return here on his own, I'd bought us some time.

"Are we really doing this? What are we even looking for?" Marius asked me with a sideways look towards Lyra, to check how her French learning was really going. She'd already switched off and strolled into the apartment as soon as I'd got the door open.

"I'm not sure, but we can always ask," I said, before switching to English and calling out to Lyra. "Lyra, can you think of anything Ursula might have given to Fern recently? Maybe a present, or something like that?"

"Presents? Ursula?" Lyra nearly laughed before remembering the seriousness of the situation. "No, she's not exactly the warm and fuzzy giving type. I can't see her willingly parting with anything, aside from information - asked and unasked for." Lyra's expression cleared for a moment - a sign that I recognised as inspiration striking. "Come to think of it, Fern was asking around for an English speaking dentist in the local area a week or so ago. She wanted recommendations. Maybe Ursula passed something on. She asked me, too - saying she wanted to research the best one - but I've been popping back to England for that."

"Thanks," I said, wandering through to the kitchen. A vision of a dentist's card attached to the fridge swam in my head, before I found it again.

Dr. Hans Schmeical, Cosmetic Dentistry
Guéret 3429
711 209 467

I took the cream card from the fridge, flipping it over in my fingers as I did so. It was a simple thing, designed only to inform about the name and role of the person listed and the bare minimum contact details needed to get in touch. There was nothing printed on the back of the card, but a message had been added in pen - and I thought I could guess who had written it.

Let's just say he had his 'Hans' all over me, if you know what I mean! Let me know if you enjoy your visit to the dentist as much as I do! XOXO

My eyebrows shot up. I hadn't seen examples of everyone's handwriting, but I would be willing to stake money that this particular sample belonged to Ursula. It would certainly explain why she'd been so desperate to take back what she had given to Fern. It was pretty compelling evidence that she was cheating on her husband - and who knew what would happen if he were to find out?

A question danced in the back of my mind, as I suddenly wondered if Fern had been holding onto the card with its incriminating writing on it for a reason - one that might have involved using it against Ursula. Alex had said that Fern had worked as a journalist, so manipulating information to her advantage would have come easily to her. However, I wasn't sure why Fern would have suddenly decided to conspire against Ursula - and if she had been blackmailing her for an unknown reason, pinning the evidence to the fridge was not a very secure hiding place.

I decided it was far more likely that Ursula was concerned that her little note would be spotted by the gendarmes, and that they would get her into trouble by saying the wrong thing in front of her husband. I suddenly recalled the time when Ursula had turned up at my house and how concerned she'd been when she'd asked about the gendarmes searching Fern's apartment. Now I thought I had the answer as to why in my hand.

I called Marius over and showed him the card, translating the message and telling him I strongly suspected that Ursula was the one who'd written it.

"What does it mean?" the chief of police asked, his forehead creasing in such a way that I despaired about his love life prospects, if he didn't understand simple innuendo. I'd translated it far more literally, too.

"I'm going to go out on a limb and guess that when we find this Doctor Schmeical, he will not be hideously ugly." I waited a beat for the realisation to dawn. It didn't. "Oh, come on! That was easy!"

"Are you coming to her funeral?" Lyra asked, popping back into the kitchen after standing in the main room, lost in thought, while Marius and I had been doing a spot of investigating.

I hesitated a bit before answering. "Well, I never actually met Fern," I said as gently as I could. "I don't know that it would be appropriate for me to be there. Some might consider it gawking."

"I suppose I hadn't thought about that," Lyra said, looking troubled for a moment. "Of course this kind of death attracts the weirdos. I should have known that. It always happens in the books I read. In fact, police often stake out funerals in order to see who comes - in case the killer turns up!"

I nodded but didn't point out that - given the close knit group at the heart of this case - it would be very likely for the killer to turn up at Fern's funeral and not be conspicuous for doing so.

"But you're one of us now, and you've been helping everyone get through this, so it would make sense for you to be there. We all know you're not trying to get involved because of some weird fascination with murders. That would be silly!" Lyra said.

"It would be silly, wouldn't it?" I echoed, thinking about what Marius and I were up to right this second and my history of being involved with murders, which would probably be classed as a weird fascination by some.

"Anyway, I wouldn't judge anyone who is fascinated by death. Fern and I both love all of that. Loved," she corrected, suddenly looking devastated. "Oh, it's so hard, isn't it - to just have to accept a person is locked in the past, and you'll never get to make new memories with them? They're simply… gone."

I nodded, resting an understanding hand on her shoulder. "We should probably go. I think Marius and I have checked the security as much as we can."

"Oh, look at all of this!" Lyra said, stopping by the computer nook and staring at the shelf of crime novels. "I really will miss our shared love of crime." She sighed. "Maybe I should start listening to that podcast she enjoyed so much. I wonder what the last one she ever listened to was about? Her last podcast… it's strange to think that way. Did you find the thing that Ursula gave to Fern?" she asked abruptly - filling me with alarm that she might not be as other planetary as the impression she gave.

"I think so. It was a card for a cosmetic dentist. I suppose Fern must have been interested in going in for something other than a regular checkup," I said - simultaneously recalling Ursula's pearly teeth and deciding that whitening had probably been the foundation for her relationship with Doctor Schmeical.

"That's strange. I was actually jealous of how white and straight Fern's teeth were. I'm not surprised that Ursula has had work done," Lyra added with a slight scoff. "That woman…" She trailed off and shook her head. "Let's just say I don't think she's trying to look good for the benefit of her husband."

"I did get that impression," I commented, thinking of the note that had been left on the card. I suddenly wondered if Alex had happened upon the same note and had drawn a terrible (and incorrect) conclusion that had driven him to murder, but I shook the thought away as soon as I had it. The first thing even the most simple minded of murderers would have done would be to pop the incriminating evidence in the bin, as opposed to leaving it in plain sight on a refrigerator. And this murderer was anything but simple minded.

"Do you want the dentist or the podcast?" I asked Marius when we were back outside of the apartment and Lyra had left.

He didn't look enthusiastic about either option.

"I would have thought a podcast, where amateurs presumably attempt to solve cold cases, would have appealed to the critic inside of you," I said, only just managing to keep my eyes from rolling.

"I do like criticising people who try to do jobs they aren't qualified for," he agreed - without a trace of irony. "I've had to put up with that sort of thing before. A cat went missing and one local busybody must have read too much *Miss Marple*. She decided it was her case and that she would play detective… and people actually tipped her off and helped her! Instead of me - the actual local police agent!"

I waited for him to draw the parallels between what he was complaining about and what we were up to right this second.

No pennies dropped.

"Enjoy your podcast," I said, giving up all hope of Marius ever showing something like self-reflection.

"Oh, I will," he agreed emphatically, a smile jumping onto his lips. "Enjoy your trip to the dentist… but not too much," he added with a slight frown, showing that at least a few of the details hadn't passed him by entirely.

"Oh, I will," I said with a big grin, mirroring back his own enthusiasm.

Marius' smile vanished. "I hope he has bad… everything."

11

SECRET SMILES

Doctor Hans Schmeical certainly didn't have bad everything. In fact, he didn't seem to have bad anything.

I studied the larger than life poster of the man himself on the wall behind the receptionist's desk and reflected that I could see why Ursula might have been tempted away from Derek, if love was a competition based on looks alone. The man in the picture had dark blonde hair that had been stylishly side-parted, a reassuringly white and straight smile, and the sort of sculpted cheek bones that would make a casual onlooker assume they were looking at a professional model, not the dentist himself. Only the caption on the image had given away his identity.

"He won't be long. I'm sure he'll be happy to squeeze you in between appointments. We are always ready to help clients who might struggle with the language barrier at other local cosmetic specialists. That's just one of the great things about Hans… he's so linguistically talented that he can speak five different languages completely fluently." The receptionist shook her perky blonde ponytail. "I just don't know where he finds the time to do all of that, while also keeping a quarter of Creuse smiling. He amazes me more every day."

"I see," I said, taken aback by the hype this young woman was heaping on her employer. I wondered if it was something she'd been asked to say to any prospective new client whilst they waited in the blue and white waiting room. The modern space featured magazines that weren't several years old and toys that did not look like they'd been worn down by a thousand pairs of tiny hands. All in all, it was a far cry from the dentists I was familiar with. *But Hans Schmeical is a cosmetic dentist,* I remembered, reflecting that this distinction may have an awful lot to do with the change of decor and the way that things were run.

I was still looking around when the door to the dentist's treatment room opened and the man himself walked out, glowing like he downed a whole carton of multivitamin juice every morning and probably followed it with a half-marathon for fun before breakfast. I was still marvelling at how someone could look so healthy, and detecting the hint of plastic beneath the initially flawless impression, when Miranda followed him out of the room.

The other woman stopped dead when she saw me, the look on her face telling me that Ursula was not the only one who might have been seeing her dentist for more than just teeth whitening. "Oh. You're here," she said, her eyes narrowing as she tried to work out why I was here - and if it was a threat to her.

I wondered if Fern had been judged in the same way.

I wondered if Miranda and Ursula had been willing to kill to keep their affairs a secret.

I decided that the best way to find out the truth was to do some truth sharing of my own… or at least, part of the truth. "Fern had a card pinned to her fridge that mentioned this dentist. I saw it when I was helping Alex out. I've been looking for a specialist dentist for a while, and it's nice to have someone who speaks your own language, isn't it?" I said, nodding to the dentist - who was otherwise engaged with the now giggly receptionist.

Miranda swept her long red hair back over her shoulders. "Yes, that's exactly why I come here," she agreed, deciding to accept my offer of saving face. "There's nothing wrong with caring about your appearance," she added, shooting me a doubt filled look that I decided not to take personally. Miranda and I were not two people that anyone would ever consider alike.

"Did you happen to see Ursula passing on Dr Schmeical's details to Fern?" I asked, taking the opportunity to try to confirm the writer of the note.

Miranda nodded. "Sure, it was on our last girls' night. Ursula loves coming here. I think she burns even more cash than I do," she added with a giggle, before covering her mouth when she remembered who she was talking to, and what she might have just implied. "I must be getting on. Nice seeing you again," she added as a throwaway remark we both knew she didn't mean, before she left the dentist's office and disappeared onto the sun-kissed street beyond.

"Ms French, how can I help you?" the dentist said as soon as Miranda had left the premises. The megawatt smile from the poster was turned towards me, and I felt momentarily stunned and in need of being cleaner somehow. This entire place would have made dust tremble in fear, and with my own renovation ongoing, dust was something that clung to me - like a misplaced toffee on the backside of an unfortunate sofa sitter.

"I'm not exactly sure... but perhaps if I explain what I know, you might be able to help me," I said, stepping towards the privacy of the treatment room and allowing the dentist to lead the way inside. And that was how I began my tentative tiptoe towards asking the dentist if he had a side hustle that involved getting up close and personal with married women… and if anyone had ever tried to blackmail him, or the women in question, over it.

There was definitely sweat beading on the back of my neck when the final question landed and a long pause followed.

"I can't comment on anything specific relating to my clients without their permission to disclose it. It's standard medical practice," the dentist said, showing that he had at least some idea of the rules that professionals were supposed to play by. The way his gaze remained fixed on the spotlights on the ceiling, whilst he evaded answering the question, made me think that my suspicions about a distinct lack of boundaries between him and the clients themselves were probably well founded.

"Did someone named Fern Higgle visit you recently?" I asked - having kept the question in reserve to change the topic swiftly after walking on such dangerously thin ice.

He rubbed his smooth chin thoughtfully. "I'm good with names and faces. I remember her coming in about a week ago. She had some questions about my clients. I told her the same thing I just told you: I can't discuss specifics of clients or treatments they may, or may not, have had."

"Do you remember who she was asking about? Was it someone female?" I suggested, knowing I was treading a fine line between asking the dentist to break confidentiality and asking him to merely repeat whatever it was that Fern had been seeking.

Dr Schmeical's expression went curiously blank for a moment, as he paused to think. All of the fillers and botox desperately smoothed everything to impossible levels of plastic perfection. "No… she was asking about a man, but I really can't say more than that."

"I see," I said, thinking that he definitely *could* have said more, he just didn't want to. Even so, I decided to put it on the back burner for now, as I had no real idea of what I was looking for, or if it was relevant to the murder.

I frowned as I tried to work out how Ursula's note - that she'd surely been trying to hide - tied in with Fern coming and asking about a man. If she'd wanted to out Ursula in some way, or blackmail the dentist himself, it was a strange approach to have taken. She could have been trying to put the cat among the pigeons by hinting that she was going to tell Ursula's husband, Derek, about the affair, but it was an indirect route for someone who didn't need to have implied anything at all, when some pretty compelling evidence had been pinned to her fridge. "Did Fern say anything else memorable?" I added, knowing that open ended questions were often the best way to find out unexpected information when you weren't sure of what you were looking for.

Dr Schmeical exhaled and ran a hand through his incredibly thick hair. "No, she just asked about... precious metals and teeth," he said, tipping his head back and forth as he inwardly decided he was being vague enough with his sharing of information.

I tried not to sigh in his face, but instead thanked him for his time and left the sparkling office with more questions than I'd entered with. I'd been expecting the evidence to begin to stack up against Ursula, but unless Dr Schmeical had been lying to cover up his part in all of this, it would appear that I'd been barking up the wrong tree. *But why would Fern have wanted to know about a male client?* I wondered, trying to decide if the deceased had been up to something that had ultimately put her life in danger, or if she'd merely seen some work she wanted to get done herself, and this whole avenue of investigation was a wild goose chase. I bit my lip, unsure of what conclusion to draw when I didn't have enough facts to go on.

My phone beeped when I exited onto the street, following in the footsteps of the mysterious Miranda. I opened the message that had slipped through in the stronger phone signal area of Guéret and saw it was from Marius.

Come home now.
You have to see this.
I think I know why Fern was killed.

12

THE SCOOP

"Watch this," Marius said, pushing a laptop in front of me when I returned to my house and found him at the kitchen table. Three empty cups sat in front of him and a thin sheen of excitement was on his face. "This crime podcast that Fern was such a dedicated follower of shares videos in the evidence list that they put beneath every episode. Not only do the podcasters revisit cold cases, they also want their listeners to pitch in and help them to solve the crimes that the police couldn't, back when the cases were actively investigated," he explained.

"Maybe we should become fans," I commented, shooting Marius a jokey smile.

"Absolutely not," he replied, not looking amused in the slightest. "Just watch this and let me know what you think. It was part of the evidence listed beneath the episode that was released a few days before Fern died."

Sensing his nervous excitement, I got serious and zipped my lips, watching the video that had prompted Marius to send me a message saying that he believed he'd found the motive for Fern's murder. As I watched events unfolding before my eyes, I thought he might have hit the nail on the head.

The video had been taken from a CCTV camera inside a jewellery shop. Glass cases filled the room, gently illuminated by lights that were always on - theoretically to make the bright space less appealing to any would-be thieves. Whilst it may have put a casual burglar off, it hadn't dissuaded another thief... and this one had come very well equipped.

"What is that?" I marvelled out loud when the contraption came into view. It was made of poles and wires that were being operated from somewhere unseen. As I watched, the device was lowered over a central glass box that had something blurry sitting within, raised up on a plinth. A bright light flashed, and then something happened that I couldn't make out on the footage - but I would have guessed that the glass was being cut by a tool attached to the mechanism. I was on the cusp of commenting how impressive the contraption was - and how I could see why Marius was drawing the parallels between this crime and what had been done to Fern - when everything went wrong.

There was no sound on the CCTV, but when the whole device suddenly collapsed onto the glass it had been so carefully working on, I still winced when the box shattered. Immediately, a red light flashed, indicating that an alarm must have gone off. The video was transformed into a scene from a gritty film noir... which was when the thief finally put in an appearance.

"This is where it gets interesting," Marius said - just in case I'd been snoozing through this Hollywood level thriller of a video.

If the mechanical arm had been impressive and subtle, what now followed was the opposite. Whatever had gone wrong with plan A, the culprit hadn't decided to walk away and call it a day. Instead, the jewel thief had switched back to good old fashioned methods, and a smash and grab had begun in earnest. Normally, an experienced thief would have been smart enough to cover his face, or risk never fingering another jewel again, but this thief had believed that the extendable arm would do the job for him - so he hadn't covered up. Now, his identity was on full display for all who watched the CCTV footage to see.

Or it would have been, had this not been CCTV footage from the early 2000s - which meant that the definition was comparable to a self portrait done using cross-stitch.

Marius reached past me and hit pause right when the culprit was standing close to the camera with his head turned in profile and a grimace on his face. "Check it out," he said, pointing to the man's mouth. "The podcasters specialise in enhancing old CCTV footage, so this is theoretically better than what was available at the time. Even so… it's hard to make out a lot."

"There's something metallic in his mouth," I commented, impressed by Marius' observation skills.

"Derek has a gold tooth," the chief of police added, impressing me again. I silently reminded myself to not underestimate my partner in crime solving.

"Is that brown hair?" I murmured, my nose nearly touching the screen, as I tried getting closer in an attempt to see more detail than was really there, before pushing back in case distance made it better. Neither made much difference. All I could make out was the glint of gold that Marius had picked up on, the suggestion of brown, or maybe darker, hair - made impossible to judge by the red glow - and a pale line down the man's cheek that appeared to be a scar. He was dressed in a yellow T-shirt with a red and blue logo that couldn't be deciphered. There was nothing else I could take from the footage - which was probably why the police hadn't managed to solve it at the time. It was clear that this robbery had turned into a mess when the jewel stealing device had failed, but if the person responsible hadn't been stupid - and the hi-tech device would suggest not - then it would have been almost impossible to track him down, if he'd got away and no traceable evidence had been left behind.

But I wondered if Fern had managed to succeed where the police had failed.

"What do you think?" Marius said, gesturing to the screen. "The contraption and the tooth... it has to be Derek doesn't it? He ticks all of the boxes."

I sat back in my chair and looked at the frozen screen, trying to see everything objectively - trying to look at it in the same way as Fern. "She must have had something more to back up her suspicions. It's impossible to be sure that it's definitely Derek from this footage. It's true that he has a gold tooth, but there's a scar on this man's face, which I don't recall seeing on Derek - or anyone else, for that matter."

Marius shrugged. "The point is, this has to be it, doesn't it? This video is what made Fern start investigating, and then the culprit... probably Derek... found out and killed her to keep her quiet, using the same techniques he used back when this crime was committed, but more effectively."

We both looked back at the screen again. "He does make something called kinetic sculptures for a living," I said, remembering him sharing his occupation. Derek had made it sound as though he was an artist - but art meant different things to different people. Perhaps to Derek, pulling off a jewellery heist or a murder was akin to painting a perfect portrait.

Marius cleared his throat. "I listened to the whole podcast twice. To summarise, a thief robbed a jewellery shop in London, called Precious Pebbles. There was a special exhibition at the time of a robbery, featuring jewels that were normally kept in a private collection. The star of the exhibit was a unique diamond ring. It featured a black diamond with crimson depths that, according to the podcast, even experts in the field couldn't explain. Even though the camera picked up the thief and the alarm was triggered, he still got away with everything he'd come for... and no further clue or trace of the culprit, or any potential accomplices, was ever found. The case was closed years later on the grounds of a lack of evidence."

"You listened to it... in English?" I said, suddenly realising that Marius sounded very knowledgeable about all of this, considering that the podcasters were from England.

Marius frowned. "I know some English. What of it? That doesn't mean I like using it," he muttered, refusing to take any sort of compliment that might have been coming next.

I decided to let Marius' weird reaction go and glanced back at the screen, minimising the video to return to the main podcast page. "I wonder if we're right about this," I mused, knowing that just an hour earlier, I'd been chasing a completely different angle. "Fern must have known something that we don't," I added. "But if she did, then did she keep any evidence that she'd uncovered... and how did the killer find out about her suspicions?"

We lapsed into a thoughtful silence as nothing jumped out. "Alex mentioned that Fern liked to do everything by herself, so that she would get full credit, don't you remember? She worked as a journalist. She might have been secretive with the things she'd found out, because she didn't want anyone else to take her scoop." I glanced at the screen again. "Or in this case... she didn't want anyone to take away her chance of getting onto her favourite podcast." I sighed, silently thinking that there was a strong chance - going by the short time between the podcast's launch and Fern's death - that Fern hadn't gathered much actual information at all, and had instead been in the process of getting started when the murderer had realised what she was doing and taken early preventative action. Fern might have asked the wrong question of the wrong person... and she'd ended up dead.

...The same questions that Marius and I were beginning to ask.

I bit my lip and looked despondently at Marius, knowing that we were still in the dark. "Something must have tipped off the killer to be on alert," I said, clutching at a fresh straw.

"Maybe they knew about the podcast. Lyra was talkative enough to let us know about it," Marius suggested.

I nodded. "That, or they could have been savvy enough to set up a Google alert."

Marius looked blank in the way that most people in Sellenoise did as soon as you mentioned technology.

"It's a thing that will send you a notification via email if a certain phrase pops up somewhere on the internet. For example... as part of the title of a new podcast," I said, indicating the heading, where 'Precious Pebble Robbery' was listed. "If someone here had an alert set up for that phrase, it would have tipped them off - especially if they knew that Fern listened to *Cold Case Crackers*."

"Do you think that fact alone might have been enough for them to get rid of Fern?" Marius speculated.

I considered. "She went to the dentist and asked questions, but even before that, she openly asked for recommendations... perhaps to make it seem less obvious that she was up to something. I suppose she must have been hoping that the dentist would be able to confirm whether the metallic thing in the footage is definitely a gold tooth, and if it's located in the right place to be the same as Derek's. However, Doctor Schmeical claimed that he didn't tell her anything because of client confidentiality. Miranda confirmed that Fern asked Ursula for the dental recommendation during a girls' night. She could have mentioned it to Derek when she got back home."

"And then Derek realised what was happening and finished her off, before she could finish him off by exposing his crimes on the podcast and turning him into the police," Marius announced in dramatic fashion.

"Well, possibly," I had to counter, but it did seem to be a genuine possibility, given the modus operandi and the order of events as we knew them. "I think it's time we had a chat with Derek. How about we visit him tomorrow morning?" I suggested, knowing I'd have to ask Damien for the address. At least it would make Ursula and me even, after she'd turned up on my doorstep unannounced.

"The truth will be revealed, and Jaques Laurent will also be revealed as a total loser," Marius said, unknowingly echoing the gendarme's view of him.

I opened my mouth to tell him there was no need for nastiness. Our goal was to wrap up a mystery that may otherwise languish just as long as the jewellery heist - but then I remembered how manipulative Jaques had been, and I shut it again. If there was some way to solve this case and prevent Jaques from interfering with Sellenoise and its police force ever again, I would happily seize it with both hands.

"We shall see what Derek has to say," I said, mentally preparing myself for the inevitably chatty phone conversation I would need to have with Damien in order to extract the piece of information I was after.

But as it turned out, Derek Cooper found me first.

13

A RISKY RECOMMENDATION

"Knock knock!" someone called out bright and early the following morning - instead of actually knocking on the door.

I stopped stirring my tea and frowned, recognising the voice immediately as belonging to one of the people I'd planned to pay a visit. A chill ran up my spine. I suddenly wondered if, just as Fern's investigation had been cut short, my own had been detected and was about to reach a very sudden end. Then, I countered that thought with the knowledge that Fern's death had been swift, as a sort of damage control that the person responsible had hoped would never be traced back to them, or their past. Now, a different game was afoot - although that didn't mean I should let my guard down.

Spice whined and looked at me from the sofa, asking if I was going to answer the door, or let the strange singsong knocking continue.

"If I don't come back, tell Marius whodunnit," I said to the dog, who promptly shut his eyes again and went back to sleep. Spice clearly thought I was being overdramatic.

I wrapped my dressing gown more tightly around me and silently wondered if I should consider going to bed fully dressed to avoid situations like this.

"Did you forget our appointment?" Ursula asked when I answered the door, shooting my attire a deeply unimpressed look. Derek was standing on the doorstep next to her, looking about as enthusiastic as I felt about this situation.

"We didn't have an appointment. I've already told you that I can't take you on as a therapy client. It's a conflict of interest and I can't keep the confidentiality clause," I said, tired of listing this disclaimer over and over again with no one actually listening to me.

Ursula waved a hand to show that she didn't care, grabbing her husband's arm and swanning straight past me into my house, which she didn't hesitate to wrinkle her nose at. "Can't we just consider this a coffee time meeting between friends? I need someone to vent to, and you can throw in some couples therapy. Derek needs to up his game."

"Was that who Fern was? Someone you could vent to?" I asked, figuring that I'd given her more than enough warnings about confidentiality and conflicts of interest.

"We took it in turns," she replied, walking into the living room without asking. I followed her and was in time to see Spice slinking up the stairs that led to the bedroom above - sensing that Ursula was not likely to be an animal lover. "You know what it's like living out here. Fern had her annoyances in life, and I have mine. Our friendship worked very well."

"Well enough for you to recommend a particular dentist to her?" I suggested, keeping an eye on Derek when I said it.

But it was Ursula who reacted.

She froze and turned to me with fear flashing in her eyes, glancing across at her mute husband, before returning her gaze to me. "Look… I don't know what you think you know, but some things that are said, or passed, between friends after a few glasses of wine might have given an entirely incorrect impression."

"Fern took the recommendation seriously enough to visit the dentist in question," I said, keeping one eye on Derek as I spoke. I was hoping to see a telltale sign that this was what had got Fern into trouble and tipped him off that his identity and crimes were about to be revealed. *That's if he's guilty,* I reminded myself, aware that I was several pieces short of completing the puzzle.

"That thing I wrote was a joke between ladies, or does your training in psychotherapy not extend to humour?" Ursula hissed.

Derek remained as animated as a plank of wood. He was either a masterful actor, or had no idea about what we were discussing.

"Look… everyone wants whiter teeth!" Ursula continued, desperate to fill the silence I'd deliberately left. "I don't know what you think you know, but it really was just an innocent referral. Everyone wants a whiter smile - especially when they're trying to keep a fish on the end of a hook," she said, doubling down on her denial of there being anything more than dentistry between her and Dr Schmeical, while simultaneously trying to push my attention in a new direction.

"You mean Alex?" I asked, deciding to allow Ursula to lead me in this direction. Her husband didn't seem keen to engage in the conversation. I'd watched every move he'd made since following us into the living room, but the only sign of animation he'd shown had been when he'd spotted a simple desktop toy I kept on the fireplace, where steel balls bounced into each other.

Ursula's smile was victorious as she seized the opportunity to change the subject. "I don't want to cause any trouble, but Fern wasn't the only one interested in Alex when he first joined our little group. Maybe he regretted his proposal and couldn't think of a way out of it, or maybe the woman who'd been forced to watch their romance unfold from the sidelines finally snapped and used her knowledge of mechanics to make a killing machine. I'm talking about Lyra," she added, in case she hadn't been obvious enough.

"I see," I said, taking everything Ursula had just said with a very big pinch of salt. She was seeking to stir the pot, and a good reason for that would be that she wanted her own exposed secrets to be covered up by the possible misdemeanours of others.

"I've been wondering a lot about what happened to Fern - may she rest in peace," Ursula added in the afterthought manner of someone who is hoping to win brownie points for saying that they care, but whose sentiment has the same amount of calculation behind it as a politician's speech. "I've found myself the subject of much scrutiny, courtesy of someone telling the gendarmes about that unfortunate misunderstanding with the house key." She meant the time when she'd broken in to Alex and Fern's apartment to try to get back the business card that had been pinned to the fridge. "It's ridiculous that they're focusing on me, when the person who set up the trap with the axe thing would have known what they were doing, wouldn't they? That obviously excludes me! I don't know the first thing about mechanics, or making things. But Alex or Lyra…"

"Derek's pretty good at making things, isn't he?" I said, glancing over at the quiet man, who finally looked up at the mention of his name.

"I'm an artist, not an engineer," he said airily.

Ursula shook her head. "I get to hear those words every time I want something fixed in the house. With his artistic ideals always coming first, it's a wonder that we can keep a roof over our heads. Well, it *would* be a wonder… if I wasn't funding everything!"

THE FRENCH FIASCO

"I have standards," Derek said, apparently paying more attention than he appeared to be.

"Standards that stopped you from accepting a highly paid commission from a super shopping centre in Paris, who wanted you to make them a custom kinetic sculpture," Ursula raged.

"I don't believe in consumerism," Derek said, moving to stare out of the window. His wife's hands twitched in such a way that made me think she was probably considering strangling him.

My eyes returned to Derek for several moments, as I tried to work out if this entire impromptu not-therapy session had been devised by the strange pair to throw me off the scent. I was usually pretty good at spotting liars, but in this case, I genuinely had no idea what was going on. "How did you two meet?" I asked, tentatively trying to find out how such an unlikely pair had found each other and ended up together.

"We crossed professional paths," Derek answered with a mysterious smile that pushed me back towards wondering if I was being toyed with. Ursula worked in jewellery sales, and Derek may have been responsible for stealing some. Perhaps his wife's insider knowledge had been instrumental in pulling off the heist. Many successful robberies were aided by someone who worked within the targeted business or organisation. Ursula might have handed Derek the jewels on a platter and somehow fallen for him at the same time.

It was the second part that I found harder to reconcile than the first.

"Stop being so mysterious, Derek. We're not lovestruck teenagers trying to make out that we have a romantic backstory," Ursula chided. "We did meet professionally… at an exhibition where Derek was showing his sculptures and I was networking with jewellery makers - hoping to scout some new talent." She sighed. "Back then, I suppose I was taken with Derek's sincerity and passion for his work, and one thing surprisingly led to another. People do say that love is blind," Ursula said with an astonishing lack of subtlety, given that her husband was standing right in front of her.

"Dearest, I know you like to put on a reluctant face in front of outsiders, but you love me really. We're very happy," Derek said, directing the last part at me.

"I'd be happier if you actually paid some attention to me, instead of your ridiculous contraptions!" Ursula bit back.

"I'm working on a big project right now! Once it's sold to someone who will appreciate it, we'll have all the time in the world to do whatever you want, my love," Derek said, his eyes widening and focusing on Ursula in an adoring fashion. He only spoiled it a bit by grumbling under his breath about giant superstores with lots of money, but no taste.

She drew herself up taller and shot him a stern look. "You'd better, or I'll be getting a divorce."

"As you say, my dear," Derek said, back to being vague - and not apparently taking his wife at all seriously. I suddenly wondered about Ursula's note, and whether there really was something going on between Ursula and the dentist, or if she'd deliberately written the scandalous note to Fern, hoping it would get back to her husband... and perhaps prompt him to focus on her a little more. When Fern had been murdered and the gendarmes dispatched to search her apartment, she might have feared that it would be seen as something serious, which was why she'd desperately tried to get it back. Possibilities swam through my brain, but I felt no closer to the truth.

As a therapist, I was used to dysfunctional relationships and couples that shouldn't work on paper, but somehow seemed to get along all the same. I could only assume that this was the category that Ursula and Derek fell into.

"I've just remembered I have a therapy client coming over in about five minutes' time," I said, suddenly inspired as to how to get rid of the pair - one of whom may possibly be a killer, although this meeting had been far from enlightening on that front. I squinted at Derek's face, but his straggly hair covered the place where a scar may, or may not, be.

"See, Derek? Even she has more business than she can handle. There's plenty of work around the place, if you're smart enough to go out and get it!" Ursula said, turning on her husband again and using my business as ammunition against him, whilst tossing in something that could be construed as an insult against me in the process.

"We have enough to get by, don't we? You believe in my art just as much as I do. I know you do."

"Yes… which is why it drives me crazy that you don't see any reward from it! I just wish you'd think out of the box more. It's not about the money, not really… it's about…" Ursula bit her lip and frowned. "It's about success, I suppose. I've stuck with you for this long, hoping that everything you're working on will come to fruition one day, but it hasn't so far, and I'm starting to have my doubts it ever will. For both of our sake's, Derek… when are you going to realise that your career is about as serious as a rubber chicken?" She threw her hands up in the air, before sighing again - visibly torn between the love I thought she genuinely did feel for her husband and the disdain she also felt for the business failings, of which she perceived him guilty.

"I eagerly await your suggestions about how I might improve," Derek replied, a trifle more waspishly than he previously had done.

"Not to rush anyone, but…" I interjected, uncomfortable that I was actively trying to get rid of two people who were probably in need of a good long sit down and a chat, but I had been very clear that the person to do that with could not be me.

Relief washed over me when both of my uninvited guests moved back towards the entrance to my house. I had a lot to think about and having them here - even after I'd been planning to pay them a visit anyway - was making me sweat like a turkey at Christmas.

"I hope that all of this gets sorted out very swiftly," Ursula said, spinning around in the middle of striding back towards her car. Derek had jogged ahead and was already sitting in the driver's seat. "It was horrible being interrogated when I'm totally innocent of anything to do with poor Fern. I'm glad you agree it was all a misunderstanding, Justine, and I hope that hardworking gendarme finds the real killer soon. If there's anything I can do to help him, you'll let me know, won't you?" she gushed after undergoing a complete and sudden personality transplant. Fortunately, my powers of observation were just as good, if not better, than Ursula's, and I'd already spotted the reason for this impromptu speech.

"I'll be delighted to pass along everything I've learned today, if the 'hardworking' gendarme you're talking about ever demonstrates that he's capable of making progress on his own. Just between us, I think he's used to cajoling and manipulating others into doing his job for him."

Ursula looked torn between shock and delight at what she must imagine to be my unintentional downfall. "Well, I must be going," she said, trying not to glance in the direction of the woodpile. "Can't say I agree with you on… all of that," she added, still trying for extra credit. She flipped her hand in a lazy wave and the sunlight made her rings sparkle red, white, and blue for a moment.

"Did Fern ever ask you where you got your jewellery from?" I asked, suddenly inspired.

Ursula stopped trying to walk away and returned, coming very close to me indeed and covering the middle ring set with dark stones with her hand. "Whatever you think you know, you don't. I got the ring you're talking about for myself from a local jeweller. Well, a pawnshop, if you must know. It's nothing special," she said in such a way that made me think it might be the opposite. "Urgh, why do people always ask about it?"

"Derek didn't get it for you?" I enquired, continuing like I hadn't noticed the sudden change of mood.

"No… didn't you listen to what I just said? It was me. A woman is allowed to buy herself nice things if she wants to. I don't need to have an extramarital affair in order to gain jewellery. Anyway, it was a total bargain and I've had it for years. I have no idea why Fern asked about it the last time we were together." She made a sound of disgust and stalked back to her car.

I waited for Ursula and Derek to wheel spin off the loose gravel of the track that led to my house, driving away into the bright morning - and hopefully out of my life for long enough that I could add a security system that allowed me to spot people before they arrived at my door… and lock it accordingly.

The breeze blew past in a rush of freshly cut grass that smelled like long summer days, barbecues, and get-togethers that went on until the sun dipped in the sky. I sighed, wishing that this moment of peace and nostalgia could be allowed to stretch on and on, and be the private moment of solitude I suddenly longed for. Alas, I knew that I was not alone, and there was even less chance I'd be allowed to contemplate the turning of the world when my second uninvited guest of the day inevitably joined me.

"You can come out now," I said to the pile of wood I kept at the end of the small patch of lawn in front of my house.

14

LEOPARDS AND SPOTS

Jaques Laurent straightened up and looked torn between embarrassment and suspicion. "How did you know I was there? Did… was it because…?" His eyes opened wide in the way people's tended to, when they knew enough about my past to be aware that I'd once made the mistake of claiming to be psychic. Even though I'd made it my mission to come clean to anyone who asked about that past error, there were still moments when it returned to haunt me, like a gendarme popping out from behind a wood pile.

"No, it was because there are footprints in the dust that are your size and type of boot… and also your hat was sticking out," I told him, nodding to a patch of dusty earth where grass had once grown, before reluctantly tacking on the clue that had probably been what Ursula had noticed.

Jaques glanced down. "Wow, you are good."

I didn't thank him but instead waited for him to reveal why he'd been spying on my house.

"Right… I was just here because…" He trailed off and narrowed his eyes at me, quickly getting over his embarrassment at being caught out. "…because I think you and your little police friend are investigating this murder!"

I considered pretending to be astonished and denying it, but beyond once feigning that my observations came in the form of visions, I'd never been very good at acting. "What makes you think that?" I asked, knowing that I was much better at using words to my advantage.

"What makes me think that?! What makes me think that, is that I know you've been talking to people about what happened. You've been asking questions. I know that because… because I always seem to talk to them right after you," he confessed, looking furious about that. "It's not your job. There is no room for armchair detectives on this case." He frowned at me. "I gave you the opportunity to be a part of this and you turned me down. What does it say that you're continuing to investigate behind my back? Are you trying to prove you're better than me, or that the gendarmes can't solve this murder? Does it make you feel good about yourself?"

I listened to everything he said, taking it all in and waiting for Jaques to feel better. I often found that letting someone fully voice their grievances in one big rush not only had the benefit of getting them to share what was really bothering them, it also allowed words that the person themselves may not have been aware they'd been holding onto to slip out. "I've always wanted you to solve this murder," I said, looking at him seriously. "I don't mean to get involved, but it is important to me that justice is done."

"It's important to me, too!" Jaques argued, looking hurt.

"I believe you," I told him, observing that - even though he had a twisted way of going about it - he genuinely did seem to care about solving this case. After all, would someone who didn't care at all be stalking me to make sure I wasn't getting the upper hand in the investigation? It was not the most linear approach, but it did show a strange kind of dedication.

"I wanted you to work with me. I still don't understand why you refused."

I looked at Jaques seriously. "Are you sure you don't understand why?" It was always best to try to let people work things out for themselves.

His expression clouded and he became silent. Whilst I was waiting for whatever revelation may occur, I invited him inside and offered him some tea, placing a plate of biscuits down in front of him.

He was halfway through a custard cream that Damien had gifted me from his 'all things English' hamper when he finally spoke. "You were upset when I said something about the chief of local police." His face screwed up as he tried to think. "Marius," he finally managed, not impressing me with his attention to detail. "I never meant to step on any toes."

"You didn't just step on my toes... you stomped on them when you insulted him, and by extension, me," I told him, tired of waiting for Jaques to crawl towards the right answer when he was surely being wilfully oblivious.

"I was hasty making judgements about other branches of law enforcement when I was not in possession of the full facts," he said, showing me he'd missed out on a glittering career in politics, where he'd undoubtedly talk a good game... and be about as effective as he was as a gendarme.

"You mean you didn't know we were friends," I corrected him with a thin-lipped smile. "Look, we clearly disagree on the best way to work with others, but I do want justice to be done, and us fighting is not going to be conducive to that. I propose a truce, and that we share anything we think might be important." I tilted my head. "Or just share anything that comes to mind," I added, knowing that sometimes the obvious could be right in front of a person's eyes and still remain invisible or misunderstood.

"Fine," Jaques agreed after a few beats of silent consideration had passed. "You go first."

I took a sip of my tea, tipping my cup back far enough that I could roll my eyes without being observed. Then, I put aside my pride and told him everything I'd learned so far.

Well, most of it anyway.

"I don't think Ursula or Derek had anything to do with it," Jaques said out of the blue.

"Oh?" I prompted, waiting for the brilliant deduction that needed to follow such a claim.

"I've spoken to her a lot… too much," he said with an exasperated look I could actually empathise with. "I don't think she sees much beyond the end of her own nose, and Derek has no killer instinct at all. Murdering Fern would be out of character for either of them."

I sighed silently. "Whilst I agree with you that Ursula is self-interested in the extreme, an out of character move can be prompted by external events that push someone to do something that does not fit their usual pattern."

"Yes, I know that," Jaques said, looking annoyed. "Also, Ursula showed me that she was planning to start a joint venture with Fern and already had some significant capital tied up in it, which legally belonged to the pair of them. The venture was only agreed a few weeks ago - a jewellery selling site that Fern was going to use her journalism expertise to promote to her old contacts in the press. I looked, but I couldn't find anything in it that would indicate a motive for murder. If anything, Fern's death is very inconvenient for Ursula, as it may well result in the failure of the business plan."

"Thanks for sharing," I said - although, not without the sarcasm it deserved after how grudgingly Jaques had spoken.

I'd already told him about the note on the dentist's card, and how Ursula and Miranda were potentially both going to the dentist for more than teeth whitening with Dr Schmeical. I'd also mentioned the podcast, but beyond telling him to take a look at it and the CCTV footage, I hadn't contributed any opinions. It was up to Jaques to decide which one he thought was the most compelling motive for murder.

"I interviewed Henry and Miranda recently. Henry does odd jobs, but mostly seems to stay home, and Miranda travels more often than not to work with the leaders of fashion when they need extra support staff. I suppose that sort of thing might have led to infidelity, but I don't see how it would connect to the murder. Miranda seems to specialise in organising events and exhibitions for trendsetters - not designing mechanically brilliant boobytraps," Jaques said, shrugging as he shared his opinion of the expat group's other couple. "Of course, there is someone who works professionally in the field of mechanical engineering..."

"Lyra," I acknowledged, but shook my head. I hadn't been able to find a motive, beyond the tenuous one that she'd wanted Alex for herself. The problem with that theory was that Fern and Alex had been together long enough to get engaged. I couldn't see why she would have decided to act now.

"Justine, I do think we have far more in common than you realise," Jaques said when we'd finished moving our respective chess pieces around the board. "I also want you to know that I believe you're incredibly capable. I really did hope that you working with me on this case might have led to us getting closer to one another." His eyes were wide and searching, looking for a reaction that I was willing to bet quite a lot of women gave him quite a lot of the time.

"It's always nice to know I'm considered capable," I replied, not letting my own frost melt. "While this particular case is problematic, given my position as a witness, if you do need help with future cases, maybe it would be a good idea for you to ask for it," I said, thinking about how much fuss that would have avoided in the past. No more sneaking around, and no more wondering how the gendarmes were getting on and what they might actually be doing - if anything.

"I don't know how much need there'll be for a translator in future cases - unless your Brit friends are planning to make a habit of this?" Jaques replied, deliberately misunderstanding my offer.

I shot him a disparaging look that summed up the skepticism I felt towards every single honeyed word he'd said to me prior to now. A leopard could no sooner change its spots than Jaques could conceal his disdain of rural life and those who lived it. "Good luck with solving the murder. I'm sure it's almost in the bag," I said, standing and indicating that I'd had my fill of the gendarme and his empty words.

He stood reluctantly, apparently only now realising that he'd said too much once again. "Thank you for sharing with me today. I really am doing everything I can to solve this case," he said, trying to claw back some good feeling between us.

I surveyed him for a long moment. "Unfortunately, I think you probably are," I observed, shutting the door behind him and saying a silent prayer that we could stay out of each others' way for some time. But unless Jaques proved me wrong about his sleuthing skills, fate probably had some other ideas about that.

Speaking of fate… or rather, fêtes… it was with stomach dropping dread that I suddenly remembered what day it was today.

15

SASH OF SHAME

"Is that what you're wearing?" Marissa greeted me when I let her in later that morning.

"What's wrong with this?" I asked, looking down at my pink shorts and flowery blouse that I'd put on after my dressing-gown-clad meeting with far too many people far too early in the morning.

Marissa threw my ensemble a look that heavily implied there was a good reason I was still single, and she was looking at it. "Nothing's wrong with it," she lied. "But also… maybe you could wear a dress? Everyone likes a dress. It shows you've made a bit of an effort."

"What sort of dress did you have in mind… something white, frilly, and with a lengthy train at the back?"

"Don't be silly, that sounds over the top," Marissa said, without a hint of humour.

I wondered if I should point out that I was being facetious, but decided that the other woman had missed my joke deliberately. She wasn't going to laugh at her friend's brilliant sense of humour until I'd put on a different outfit. Feeling like the gawky teenager in a film, prior to their prom transformation - when all the bullies suddenly decide that the total loser scrubs up pretty well after all, and is by some twisted logic, someone they should now treat like a human being - I stalked into the living room, up the stairs, and into the vast bedroom beyond. I threw open the isolated second-hand wardrobe, that looked like it might possibly contain Narnia, and flicked through the items of clothing hanging up, grumbling about an event I'd never said I'd attend. In the end, I found a fuchsia jersey-knit wrap dress with a neat buckle at the waist. To me, it looked like it would be worn by someone who'd made more effort than was necessary to buy groceries, and less effort than a person desperate to hook a date at something awful called Singles Celebration Day.

I walked back down the stairs and entered the kitchen, spreading my arms wide for approval. If I'd been expecting applause, or even appreciation, I was disappointed.

Marissa sighed. "I suppose it's an improvement. It's better than your previous supermarket shopping outfit, but not exactly right for a date."

"Exactly!" I agreed, pleased we were on the same page about the outfit.

Marissa's expression strongly suggested that we weren't. This became even more apparent when she whipped out a sash she'd been hiding behind her back all this time.

"Wait... when you said everyone would be wearing an identifying symbol, I thought you meant a badge, or... or a flower pinned to the lapel!" I said, my jaw dropping in horror.

"Justine, today is a day to be loud and proud... not shy and subtle," Marissa chided, approaching me like I was a nervous pony who might bolt any second.

"You know I don't want to do this!" I complained after losing the small wrestling bout that had followed. Marissa was formidable when she wanted something. "Wait... why is this in English?" I asked, reading the slogan that had been printed on the beauty pageant style wrapping. "Single and ready to mingle?!" I quoted incredulously.

"We'll be late. Let's go," Marissa said, bundling me towards the door when she sensed further resistance.

"Did I ever tell you how much I loathe and despise you?" I said when she was frogmarching me down the hill towards the town square.

"Come on, it will all be over and done with soon."

"What happened to 'you might enjoy it'?" I asked, noticing how Marissa's words had shifted.

The town square looked distressingly busy when we approached. I had hoped that only eligible bachelors and bachelorettes would be invited to this ritualistic single shaming event, but it would appear that I was participating in a spectator sport.

"Justine's here, everyone!" Marissa yelled when we reached the edge of the crowd.

"I am going to kill you," I hissed at her, wishing I could run back up the hill and hide in my house. Normally, I loved social occasions and joining in with the town spirit, but this was different… very different.

"Marius would have to arrest you if you did that… or would it be the job of that handsome gendarme who handles the serious crimes around here? If you'd brought him here as your date, you could have ditched the sash," Marissa whispered back, the smile never leaving her lips.

"I can't believe that you think this is funny," I said, knowing that Marissa had needed a star attraction for her event - some fresh meat for the annual bash. "You're supposed to be buttering me up, not making jokes. Wait - which one did you think I should have invited as a date?" I asked, suddenly aware that her words could be interpreted in two different ways.

"Must dash, I need to take care of the nibbles. Have fun!" Marissa said, giving my shoulder a squeeze and shooting me an evil smile that did not answer my question at all, before slipping away into the throng of people - most of whom were sashless.

"I will get you for this," I promised in a very un-me-like way, wondering if I could get away with screwing up the sash and throwing it in a bin before things could become any worse. I was totally in favour of there being no stigma attached to being single and on the look out for love. We lived in a place where the internet and phones were unreliable, meaning that more traditional methods of romantic intervention were all that was available, but the participants should be willing. I was absolutely the opposite of willing because I liked to do things like romance on my own terms. At least, that's what I told myself when I momentarily contemplated my complete absence of anything resembling romance for an amount of time that could kindly be referred to as a dry patch, and less kindly as a distant desert planet where no life could survive.

"My dear Justine! Had I known you were going to be here, I'd have worn my best bowtie," Damien said, materialising in front of me and spreading his arms wide to show off the 'single and ready to mingle' sash he was wearing. "I never come to this event to do anything beyond showing my support, of course," he confided. "One has to get the numbers up. I have no doubt that you are here to show the same goodwill?"

"Yes, that's right," I said, feeling mollified after inwardly concocting all kinds of plans of revenge against Marissa.

"I don't know that any successful matches have ever been made," Damien said, cheerfully waving to a cluster of locals - who shot him wary looks and nodded back, just to get him to stop. I didn't like to ask whether that had always been the way, due to his eccentric behaviour, or if the latest murder had brought him some extra notoriety. Whatever it may be, it was water off of a duck's back to Damien, who didn't seem to notice. "Nevertheless, the event persists, and at least it gives everyone who might not have been coerced into wearing a sash of shame the chance to see who else is available. You never know... perhaps some of us might find others willing to share some good years together," he said, winking at a group of older ladies, who giggled amongst themselves. Apparently Damien's reputation wasn't completely prohibitive after all. I could only hope that my own reputation wasn't suffering in the same way - especially when I needed the town's trust, if my therapy business was going to continue to succeed.

The sound of loud and sudden laughter drew my attention away from Damien. Marius was bent double over a hay bale that was serving as extra seating, pointing at me whilst lost in hysterics - just so there could be no mistake as to what he was laughing about.

"How long until this is over?" I asked Damien, already fed up.

"It's not all bad! There's a free barbecue, and the singletons get to go first. I know it's out of pity, but isn't it best to get the free burgers while they're hot and fresh?"

"Normally, you would have had me at 'going first at a free barbecue', but for once, I don't think the food is worth the fee paid with dignity," I said, still trying to ignore Marius - who was now kicking his legs in the air.

"What's a little ritual humiliation amongst friends?" Damien said, winking at me before clearing his throat. "I've heard your house is coming along marvellously. Well done! You won't believe how many people I know that moved into falling down properties, only to still be living in little more than a hovel years later. I used to say that Creuse is where the dream of a new life in France goes to die, but you are doing so well! I would love to see how you're getting on with it all."

"You know you're always very welcome to drop by. You're the busy one of the two of us," I told him with a smile. "There's still a long way to go, but I think all of the leaks have been plugged, and this winter may not feel as cold as the last - so by those standards, I'm living in luxury."

Damien laughed. "I'm sure you're being far too modest. I remember when I was doing up my own house. It's such a wonderful feeling of accomplishment when you do a lot of it yourself, isn't it? Some people's solution is to throw money at the problem until it goes away. There's nothing wrong with that, but I do feel it lacks heart. Henry and Miranda's place is a prime example of that. They stayed with me whilst it was all being done, which is actually how I got to know them. They bought a barn for the price of a packet of crisps, the way I understand it, and then Henry threw cash at all of the local tradespeople and they got the job done in no time. It looks nice... clinical... but nice. Like something you could order out of a catalogue, which I suppose they sort of did. I just wonder why they went to all of that bother instead of buying an already done property, but at the end of the day, it's what you're happy with that matters, isn't it? Lyra's still living without running water, would you believe. She bought her house years ago, but never seems to find the time to change anything. You see what I mean?"

"I do," I agreed thinking of how I'd won my house and swiftly come to realise exactly why it had been given away and the mammoth nature of the task facing me.

"Whilst I have you here with me, I wanted to ask if you'll be joining us for the funeral tomorrow? There's going to be a wake held afterwards, so perhaps just that, if you would feel more comfortable that way. I offered my house as the venue, thinking that someone would come up with something else, because it somehow feels in poor taste." We were both silent for a moment as we reflected on the appropriateness of holding a celebration of life at the same place where the person had met their end in such a violent - and as yet unsolved - manner. "However, it would seem that there is nowhere that can be hired at such short notice, and my place is the only property that's any good for entertaining large groups, as I built it with that in mind. I do hope Fern will forgive us, but who knows? Perhaps revisiting the scene of the crime will be enough to make someone feel guilty enough to step forward and confess their sins. One can always hope."

I decided not to comment on the likelihood of that happening - which was practically zilch, considering the great pains the person responsible for Fern's death had gone to in order to conceal their crime and cover their involvement. "I don't think it would be right for me to go to the funeral," I said, thinking about what I'd said to Lyra about gawkers. "However, if you think I would be welcome, I will come to the wake," I allowed, thinking that it would give me another chance to scrutinise the suspects.

"Excellent! You'll be very welcome. The entire group is very taken with you - although, some of them are disappointed that you can't take them on as therapy clients. What a shame, eh?" he said, shaking his head. "I do hope the gendarmes sort this mess out soon. It makes one rather unsettled to think that someone amongst one's own friends could be capable of doing a thing like that. Do you know if they're zeroing in on any suspects? No one's paid much attention to me throughout this - even though it happened in my barn, I know how my weapons function, and I also had prior knowledge that Fern would be alone in the barn, because it's what she does every year. I could have set the trap up at my leisure."

I was uncomfortably reminded that Damien was rather good at tinkering and coming up with unconventional weapons. He'd once given me some homemade bombs, which had proved rather more powerful than I'd been expecting. On paper, Damien did fit the bill in many ways. The only thing lacking was a motive. "Did you do it?" I asked, just on the off chance.

"No! I can't be reducing my social circle like that! It's hard to recruit expats around here when there aren't many of us. Of course, I do also socialise with our lovely local community, but their sense of humour…" he pulled a face "…well, it's just not the same, is it?"

"Oh, I don't know… some people certainly seem to know a joke when they see one," I muttered, glancing over at where Marius was wiping his eyes after finally managing to get a grip on himself.

"How have you been getting on with your investigation?" Damien asked in a much lower voice, his eyes sparkling with curiosity.

"I'm not investigating…"

He waved a hand to cut me off. "I know you're not supposed to be, but something tells me you don't think too highly of those who are in charge of serious crimes in these parts. I've also heard that, in spite of not taking on any therapy clients for some very logical professional reasons, you've still been talking to several people who were guests at my birthday party. I know you're a very friendly person who wants to help others, Justine, but I'm also aware that you're rather sharp when it comes to seeing things the way they truly are."

"Thank you," I said, accepting the compliment and wondering how I was going to get out of commenting on the rest.

"The only thing I hope is that all of this can be wrapped

up soon - no matter who it is that manages to do the wrapping," Damien said with a small smile, after he observed my reluctance to continue down the path he wished us to saunter along. "In any case, at least you seem to be looking in the right direction. Unlike some others I could mention," he added, nodding his head towards the mairie.

I followed his gaze and suddenly realised that Damien had seen something I'd missed for once - probably because I'd been so distracted by Marius' over the top reaction. Jaques Laurent stood next to the entrance of the mairie with his hands folded at his waist, standing in the stiff manner that those who work in law enforcement seem to be born with. It was only when I looked at him that I sensed he must have been watching me all along. Even when our eyes met, he seemed intent on remaining right where he was... just watching.

"Which one of us do you think he suspects the most?" I quipped.

"Don't look at me. I've already proved far too boring for him," Damien said, almost sounding disappointed. "Maybe he's not here for the murder investigation at all," he added as he turned to walk away. "Happy Singles Celebration Day!"

16

THE WILD WAKE

"How was the funeral?" I asked Damien when I arrived at the gazebo that had been set up outside of his house on the side farthest away from the barn where Fern had met her awful end. I wasn't sure if this strategic placement was helping, or merely drew more attention to the fact that the other barn was being determinedly avoided. This piece of land could favourably be called an attempt at an orchard, and less favourably, a junk yard. Damien had often mentioned that he liked to take on projects, but it would seem that not every project reached fruition, and those that hadn't came here to die.

An old classic car of unidentified make sat rusting and in pieces, while a Union Jack sprayed set of body work languished beneath a tarpaulin. Next to them, some badly chainsaw-carved tree trunks had grown moss and mushrooms. There were also flowers, hundreds of them, scattered everywhere you looked in a riot of wild beauty, and the few trees that had flourished here had arms laden with fruit that was still ripening ready for an early autumn harvest.

"Well, no one died apart from..." Damien quipped, before

his expression sobered when he realised it was far too soon for that old joke. "It was fine. Strange, I suppose, because everyone is on edge when we're together. The day after it happened, when I had my picnic, it hadn't really sunk in. You know - that it was one of us who did it. Now, it's finally landed that the gendarmes aren't looking beyond this group for answers... and now no one wants to get too close to anyone else." He sighed. "A few people from Fern's extended family came from the UK to pay their respects, but they've already gone. It will probably be the same for many of us. People come here to start a new life, and even though we all joke about it, many of us do wish to cut ties and run away from whatever may have come before. I don't like to pry into that. Some things are best left in the past."

"Even if the past is where the real problem lies?" I asked, accidentally flipping into therapist mode when faced with someone talking about the desire to forget everything that had gone before and focus on the now. It was so often considered a positive way to look at life... and it was - to an extent. Fresh starts were great, but I knew from both personal experience, and from seeing it in others, that you'd better make sure you tied up the loose ends of your past before embarking on your great and glorious new adventure, because those loose ends had a way of tripping you up.

Whilst Damien waffled about not speaking personally, my eyes scanned those present at the wake. Derek and Ursula were keeping themselves to themselves over by an apple tree. They didn't seem to be speaking, but just stood... watching the others in a way that made me wonder if they were waiting for something. I squinted at Derek, trying once again to match up his face with that of the man who'd been caught on CCTV. It was impossible to say either way, even with my normally reliable powers of observation. Although the pair were silently drinking, Ursula's fingers drummed an anxious rhythm on the stem of the glass she held, and I noticed that her gaze seemed to be fixed on Lyra.

"Lovely day for a funeral, isn't it?" Henry said, approaching with Miranda at his side. The couple stopped by Damien and me, scanning the few others dotted around with the same careful consideration everyone seemed to be exhibiting right now.

"Well, it is the middle of the summer," Miranda countered, like he'd said something stupid instead of just inane.

"It certainly is, my love. What a scorcher!" Henry agreed, refusing to be shaken out of his positive mood. He dabbed his temple with a tissue, and I noticed a bead of sweat that stood out against his tanned skin below his sideburns, apparently resistant to being wiped.

Miranda fanned her face, looking annoyed with the way she was perspiring, which had caused the heavy makeup she wore to visibly cake. Perhaps that was the reason why she was in such a bad mood, but perhaps it was something else... like the fear of what I might say about a certain dentist in front of her husband.

I didn't get to try to pry in the same way I had with Ursula and Derek, because at that moment, we were interrupted by a late arrival.

"Where's the food?" a familiar voice said. I turned and saw Marius stroll by towards the spread Damien had put on for attendees. "What's all of this beige stuff?"

"What are you doing here?" I hissed, very aware that I'd mentioned gawkers possibly coming to the funeral. Now here was someone who fit that definition - attending a memorial for all the wrong reasons. Although, admittedly, free food was not what I'd imagined the motive to be.

"I'm here to keep an eye on everyone. The local police have a duty to keep the peace and maintain safety," he said loudly, before lowering his voice again. "I'm here to investigate with you, because that gendarme idiot and his cronies aren't getting it done. Where are they anyway?"

"They're hiding behind the hedge in an unsubtle black Mercedes, watching from a distance and imagining they're invisible, just because everyone has decided to ignore them," I told him with a sigh and a casual glance in the direction of a distant hedgerow, that was nowhere near thick enough to conceal a car. It stood out a mile away when you lived as remotely as Damien did. They'd have been better off in a tractor.

Marius sidestepped me to peer at the hedge.

"What are you doing?! Don't wave!" I said, slapping his hand down.

"They're treating this like a bad joke, so I am just treating them the same way," Marius said - fairly accurately, if truth be told. "I'm going to eat one of those strange meat cylinders in soggy pastry," he added, making a return to normal in the second half of his speech.

I stayed where I was while Henry, Miranda, and Damien drifted further away. My gaze remained fixed on the hedge and those who lurked behind it, and I wondered how sitting around doing nothing could be considered good police work.

"Looking for me?" Jaques said from behind me, having skirted the hedgerow and approached cross-country apparently in the hopes of making me jump.

"I assumed your stakeout meant you were keeping a low profile... or trying to, anyway," I said, not giving him the satisfaction of even pretending to sound surprised.

"It always pays to keep your eyes open, and people behave differently when they don't know they're being watched," he replied, getting even closer and saying it all in a quiet voice - so it might appear that we were conspiring to anyone glancing over.

"You're trying to make it look like I'm telling you something important, aren't you?" I observed, noting his body language and the way he was scanning the rest of the group - trying to indicate to watchers that something was going on. Something secretive. "Do you really imagine you'll arrive at the truth this way? Psychology will only get you so far. Pinning your hopes on the killer lashing out at me, because they imagine I know too much, is foolhardy. Hasn't this killer already proved they're wily enough to get away without being caught easily? I doubt they'd fall for such a simple trick. Not without a very compelling reason to do so."

"Excuse me, I want to say a few words," Lyra called out, tapping the side of her glass for silence.

"I think it could work," Jaques argued. "I'll keep a close eye on you, so you probably won't be killed."

"How reassuring. I have a huge amount of faith in your ability to do that," I said, my voice heavy with sarcasm. "Aren't there some important big town crimes that you and your team desperately need to solve? I want justice as much as anyone, but how much progress are you really making here?"

"How much progress are *you* making? Although - any investigation you may secretly be carrying out can be classed as obstruction of justice," Jaques warned, his shoulder brushing against mine, as he tried to move even closer and I tried to sidestep away.

"Even if Marius and I solve it and you get all the credit?" I asked dryly, knowing how these things worked. "I thought you liked people doing your job for you?"

"What I like is people respecting my authority," he growled and stalked off towards the buffet, nearly bumping into Marius when they crossed paths.

"Fern was the best friend a woman could wish for," Lyra slurred to anyone who was still listening, having overindulged in the alcoholic refreshments that Damien had supplied.

"Are you working together? Have you been lying to me?" Marius hissed as soon as Jaques was out of earshot.

I rolled my eyes, annoyed that the gendarme's transparent little ploy had worked on someone after all.

"We shared a love of many things... handsome men was one of them," Lyra said, waving her hand towards Alex - who looked like he would rather have been singled out by a sniper. "Thrillers and true crime were another thing. I always admired Fern's love of mysteries. It's almost a shame that she never turned her brilliant mind to actual crime, because she'd have been really, really good at it," Lyra continued, choking up for a moment.

I half-turned back to Marius whilst Lyra paused to collect herself. "I'm not working with him. You should trust me enough by now to know that! Honestly, it's so silly..." I added, losing control of my thoughts for a moment and letting them spill into my words.

"What's silly?" Marius hissed back, but now was definitely not the right time for me to elaborate on anything I might have been thinking or saying. Fortunately, Lyra decided to continue her meandering speech.

"My obsession has always been true crime television shows, but Fern introduced me to true crime podcasts - which she loved because the hosts always invite the listeners to do their own research and help them solve cold cases. I never got into them, because I like the more visual side of things," Lyra carried on, oblivious to the strange looks she was getting. "Seeing the victim just makes it all more real, doesn't it? But now I have the honour of picking up where Fern left off... because she was onto something." Lyra took a breath. Marius and I exchanged sharp looks, both suddenly alert. "I was minding my own business this morning in my little cottage just past the blue sign for Guéret and Sellenoise, when a mysterious envelope arrived on my doormat. When I opened it, I realised it was from Fern. It began: 'If you're reading this, something has happened to me, and this is who's responsible..."

A hush fell over the mourners, the gathering taking on the sombre mood it probably should have had from the start. There was something strange about this silence... a tension that lurked just beneath the surface.

Fern had been smarter than the killer had anticipated.

She'd discovered something... and then she'd put measures in place, in case she'd met with foul play.

Now, it would appear that the truth was going to come out without any detective work necessary.

"And? What did it say next?!" Damien burst out when Lyra didn't continue in a timely enough manner.

The tipsy woman tapped the side of her nose and laughed. "That is a secret between me and Fern. She wants me to finish what she started."

Right on cue, Jaques appeared at her elbow and began to lead Lyra away from the wake. In spite of her plucky claim, she followed the gendarme without complaint.

"That's one way to leave a party," Damien said wonderingly.

"It was certainly an exit worthy of a soap opera," I agreed, observing all of the eyes fixed on Lyra's retreat. Behind one of those transfixed pairs, a killer watched and wondered if the game was finally over.

But I thought there were still a few moves yet to be played.

* * *

"Nothing. How have we heard nothing?" Marius said as the evening drew in. He'd spent the rest of the day at my house, pacing up and down so much in my kitchen that I was starting to wonder if my newly replaced floorboards would wear out. I'd tried to reassure him that if the murderer was outed by Lyra, and she'd been persuaded to share this mysterious letter with Jaques, Damien would undoubtedly make sure he was the first to know and would dutifully spread the news. We didn't need to do anything.

"Marius, I'm sure everything is under control," I repeated, thumbing through a printed transcript of the podcast that had made the chief of police believe that he'd found the motive for murder. I wondered what Fern had written in the letter to Lyra, to be delivered in the event of her death. For most people, that sort of thing was usually left in films or in fiction, but Fern had been deeply interested in mysteries. It was rather fitting that she might have solved her own murder.

I just wished Jaques would persuade Lyra to tell him the contents of the letter she'd claimed was a secret between her and Fern. Then Marius and I could stop biting our nails, while we waited to know more.

"I mean, none of this affects us really," I reasoned, opting to remind him that we weren't supposed to be involved in this case. In fact, it was probably better for everyone if this was wrapped up neatly - courtesy of a piece of post.

Marius stopped pacing and looked at me. "Do you really want it to end this way? After everything that he's done..."

I raised my eyebrows at my police friend. "This is about a woman who was murdered. It's about bringing her killer to justice."

"I know," Marius replied, shamefaced. "That is the most important thing, of course... but he was the one who thought he could just march in and force people to pick sides… and pick people."

My eyebrows lifted even further. "You should know me better than that. There's nothing that Jaques could say to drive a wedge between us. His motives have always been completely transparent. He's someone who doubts his own ability to do the job he is theoretically qualified to do, so he instead tries to use the strengths of others to bolster him. Et voila, we find ourselves here," I finished triumphantly.

Marius looked at me like I was stupid. "I think there is something more to it than that. Especially where it concerns you and… and me," he added, his cheeks gaining some colour for a moment, before he looked away quickly and returned to pacing.

"There isn't anything going on between me and Jaques!" I protested, finally feeling forced to address the elephant in the room. "But, if there was… how would that make you feel?" I asked a lot more tentatively, feeling my heart do a few jumps in my chest and immediately wishing that I could take back the question - especially after asking it in such a therapist way.

"How does it make me feel? The thought of you working with a man who just wants to use you as a tool to help his career makes me feel furious. He doesn't care about you, Justine. Can't you see that?!"

"Yes, I can, thank you very much!" I burst out, infuriated by the way Marius was treating me like I was completely oblivious to Jaques' intentions, when I felt that he was the one who was oblivious to the real reason behind it all - which was to drive the wedge between us that I'd sworn would never be there. "If you have something to say, then say it," I said, losing my usual cool. Somewhere deep inside, I knew I was hoping for words to be said - words that I didn't quite know how I would feel if I heard them.

"Justine, I..." Marius broke off with a loud sigh. "I think all of this contact with British people has scarred me for life," he muttered, diverting into safer territory.

"I do wish you'd stop being so dramatic about..." I trailed off as something about Marius' words rang in my mind. *That's right... scars last a lifetime!* I thought, before something else that I'd seen jumped into my head. It was something that Fern would have definitely noticed... because it would have been different when she was alive. I blinked, suddenly transported back to the very first time I'd met Damien's expat friendship group.

"What... what are you talking about? What did I say?" Marius asked, perturbed by whatever expression had taken over my face.

The pieces of the puzzle falling together in my head tried to assemble themselves into words that I could use to tell Marius what had happened... and what was probably in progress right this second. "It's Lyra... I think she's in danger. I think she's put herself in danger deliberately."

"She is with the gendarmes, isn't she? I'm sure she has been persuaded to tell them what was in Fern's letter. There's no safer place for her to be."

"Lyra's not telling them anything... not when she doesn't have any proof. Fern didn't have enough proof either, but when she started asking questions - that might have led to her getting it - in front of the wrong person, it was enough for the murderer to join up the dots, faster than she could join them up herself."

Marius frowned. "But the letter..."

"Almost certainly doesn't exist," I said, deciding that Lyra's whole speech had been an act every bit as dramatic as it had appeared - because she'd taken the idea straight from the pages of a thriller. She was trying to bluff the killer. And if I was correct about it all being a fantasy, then it wouldn't be long before Jaques kicked her out of the gendarmerie for wasting his time.

And sent her straight into the clutches of the killer.

"She's attempting to find the murderer herself," I told Marius. "Lyra's trying to set a trap for the master of traps."

17

SPRINGING THE TRAP

"Should we... call Jaques?" Marius said once I'd taken him through what I thought I'd worked out, and what I thought Lyra may be trying to attempt.

I sighed as loudly and openly as I could - much to Marius' amusement. "He may be dumb muscle, but that may be exactly what we need to stop this without getting ourselves into more trouble than we can handle. Wouldn't that be nice?" I said wistfully, thinking of times when that had not been the case.

"If only I had another police agent working with me," Marius said, looking equally wistful. "Then, we wouldn't need to involve this poser."

"Pride doesn't matter when there could be a life at stake. It's all hands on deck," I said, managing to locate the business card Jaques had once given me and tapping the number into the landline.

Marius looked like he might be about to argue against us reaching out, before he nodded - showing me that, when it came to the crunch, he would always do the right thing.

"Hello? Jaques, we have a big problem. I need you to keep

Lyra…" I stopped talking when I realised that I wasn't speaking to a person, but a voicemail service. Perhaps our none too friendly conversation at the wake had been enough for him to finally stop talking to me. "Right when it actually matters!" I muttered, before leaving a hurried message I hoped would be halfway intelligible. "Write him an email!" I hissed at Marius, jabbing my finger in the direction of my laptop, in-between trying to explain everything to Jaques in a voicemail message he may never listen to.

Marius sat down at the kitchen table and clicked on my email service, tapping very quickly on the keyboard, before pressing send. I wasn't sure if I liked the slight smirk I saw on his face when I hung up after leaving my urgent message, but as long as he'd got the main point across, I could be angry with him over something in my outbox later.

"I guess we're on our own after all. At least Lyra was very careful to spell out exactly where she lives," I said, shaking my head, annoyed that I hadn't focused on it when she'd spoken about the alleged letter - whilst also signposting her location to anyone who might want to come looking for any compelling evidence she might have against them. "Do you know the blue sign she mentioned?"

Marius nodded. "It's what passes for a tourist trap around here, which probably says a lot about how few tourists we get." He cleared his throat. "Someone painted the sign that way for a joke, and then it sort of stayed as a landmark. Anyone who's lived around here for a while would know it. It marks the route between Guéret and here."

"All of the expats, who've been travelling from the direction of Guéret to Damien's house, would have seen it on their way to the party, the picnic, and the funeral," I said, realising that the sign was surely on that route. "They'd all know where to find Lyra."

"Typical," Marius muttered. "The one time we actually

want Jaques here, he's nowhere to be found." He shook his head and sighed, standing up and walking towards the door. "Out of the frying pan and into the fire."

I stopped, stunned by the translated version of a British expression that I couldn't recall using in front of Marius. But now wasn't the time to wonder if he'd secretly been swotting up on English - and why.

I had a feeling that someone had murder on their mind tonight... and this time, I wanted to be the one springing the trap.

* * *

The car's headlights picked up the blue sign fifteen minutes down the road between Sellenoise and Guéret. Marius slowed the vehicle to an idle crawl - safe in the knowledge that it was unlikely anyone was going to race past us on these quiet roads. Although, tonight, there might be more traffic on this lonely stretch than normal. Lyra had practically invited the killer to drop by to finish what they'd started with Fern. The question was... were we late, or early to the party?

"Maybe we should have just called the emergency number," Marius said when he pulled into a lay-by beyond the sign. A stone cottage was visible just over the hedge on the edge of a field. It was the sort of place that most people probably wouldn't notice, even if they'd driven past a hundred times, but Lyra had known exactly how to signpost the location... by mentioning an actual signpost.

"We could, but we'd just be tipping off the person responsible for all of this if the police came too soon, and this killer has a track record of disappearing," I said, reluctantly reminding Marius of the reason why we were jumping out of the frying pan and into the fire.

It was possible that sharing everything we'd worked out would result in a search warrant, and perhaps that would turn up something useful, but that sort of thing meant the suspect knew that the hounds were sniffing in the right direction... which gave them a chance to disappear before the pieces of the puzzle had been put together.

The gentle hum of bugs was in the evening air when we got out of the car and approached the gap in the hedge, where a gateway had been cut - just wide enough for a vehicle to pass through. It was here that we got our first prolonged look at the place Lyra called home. The grim, grey stone had been watered down by the addition of wisteria and ivy, which clambered over the walls, but it could not completely conceal what seemed to be a cheerless building - in spite of its romantically rural situation on the edge of a road as quiet as a country lane, where fields of grass and wildflowers swayed and sighed in the warm evening breeze.

"That is one ugly house," Marius said, putting it in simpler terms.

"Lyra has her eccentricities. Perhaps she sees something that others don't," I allowed, wondering if that same alternative perspective had driven her to do what she'd done. I wondered how she imagined it ending.

"There's a light on," Marius said with hope in his voice, wanting to believe that we hadn't arrived too late to do anything more than find out what had happened to Lyra.

"Her car's not here," I countered, wondering if the light had been left on as a security measure to make someone think the owner was at home, in spite of the evidence suggesting otherwise. For some, leaving a light on had become a ritual that seemed to imply that burglars were as terrified of lights, as vampires were of the breaking dawn.

I stopped and looked back at the lay-by we'd parked in. It was devoid of cars, apart from the one Marius had just parked, but it didn't feel empty. There was a presence hanging around that most people would call a gut feeling, or something sensed by intuition. I knew that gut feelings and intuition were more often based on external cues that the brain picked up on without making the conscious mind fully aware of them. In this case, the cue came in the form of the freshly overturned gravel in the lay-by that indicated someone had left fairly recently at great speed... quite possibly when they'd heard a car engine approaching from miles away and had decided to make themselves scarce. There was no sign of the car now, but I was sure it had been here. With that, the light's significance also changed, becoming a new possibility. Had it been left by someone exiting the house in a hurry, or was it there to make anyone who came looking think that something was wrong and focus on it? So they weren't concentrating on any other danger.

"Marius, stop!" I hissed the second after he'd opened the gate and taken his first step over an invisible boundary line.

"What? Oh." The way he said 'oh' and looked down at his feet let me know it was already too late.

"Nggh!" I yelled wordlessly as I crossed the distance at speed, rugby tackling his ankles and dragging him down, just as a bolt from an unseen crossbow shot past, targeted at head height. We hit the gravel hard with the tripwire tangled around my arms where it had come loose.

"You just saved my life!" the local chief of police said, looking torn between shock and awe. "I can't believe you saved... was that a rugby tackle? I didn't think you liked sport!"

I shot him a scathing look, knowing that he was referring to my less than athletic appearance. "Rest assured, I have not been concealing a secret hobby from you."

"Maybe you *should* take it up as a hobby. You have the

perfect build for..." he trailed off when he saw the way that my eyebrows had lifted and sensed danger in a way he hadn't when he'd stumbled over the tripwire "...for many pursuits. Anything you want to do," he continued, clearing his throat noisily. "What I meant to say is... thanks."

"Start with that part next time," I muttered, wondering if regretting saving someone's life was something that normally struck so soon after doing so. "It proves we're on the right track. The killer must have wanted that bolt to end up in Lyra. Or perhaps it was..." I shook my head, unable to draw further conclusions yet.

"Where is Lyra? Do you think we're too late?" Marius asked, looking around in the bewildered manner of someone who knows they were close to biting the dust but is trying to focus on what's happening in the present instead.

"The evidence would suggest that she's not here," I reminded him, gesturing to the absence of the car in the driveway, that was all but essential in this part of the country. "But we must go in to look..." I added, thinking about the tracks in the gravel from the car. There was no way to know who had been driving it, but the tripwire at the gate being active was interesting... but not foolproof. Someone else could have passed by, but been lucky enough not to stumble on it. "We should be careful and keep open minds to all possibilities - including Lyra being less clumsy than you," I said aloud.

"I am not clumsy!" Marius protested, stalking forwards, before immediately stopping when he realised what he was doing.

"At least when the gendarmes arrive there won't be any traps left for them to spring," I told him primly as I passed him, treading carefully and slowly, like I was crossing a landscape dotted with landmines, instead of approaching an aged stone cottage in the middle of absolutely nowhere.

We made slow progress. The light within the house seemed to beckon and whisper that where there was light, there was also safety. It was a lie that could prove fatal today.

Unlike the fiendish, but brilliant, set up in the barn that had spelled the end for Fern Higgle, the remotely rigged crossbow had not been a grand finale. I bit my lip, wondering if the killer had been forced to think outside of their comfort zone... or if they were actually here at all. Lyra's plan could have been more well-considered than it had initially appeared.

"Careful," I warned Marius when I looked at the front door and noticed that the knob had copper wires subtly wrapped around the place where the metal tapered. At least it reassured me that we were on the right track. There was something about this trap which whispered of the same level of neat efficiency as the plastic box covering the trigger mechanism I'd seen in the barn.

I looked around for inspiration and found it in the form of a pair of rubber wellington boots that had been left to the side of the door, caked in mud. I slipped my hands inside the boots, trying not to think about how many miles they'd covered and the state of the person's sweaty feet inside them, and managed to awkwardly turn the handle. It proved to be unlocked - although, this time, I wasn't sure that it was the owner who'd left it that way.

"Not exactly rolling out the welcome mat," Marius commented when we sidestepped past the deadly doorknob.

"That's because you aren't welcome," someone said from inside the house.

18

COSTA DEL CRIME

"You're a bit too early to find the crime scene, but I can still make this work," Henry Jones said, adjusting his grip on the large hunting rifle he had pointed between us.

"No you can't. We know who you are and what you've done," Marius scoffed, before his expression cleared. "Oh... you meant by killing us. Right," he said, impressing me by understanding that much English and being able to respond in kind - the way I'd suspected when he'd used that unusually English turn of phrase earlier this evening.

"Henry, you're going to get caught. The gendarmes know everything and are on their way here. You don't need to do this and make anything worse for yourself," I said, hoping that Marius would trust me to do the talking.

"You know, I've heard people say things like that before," Henry said, tilting his head and lifting the gun just a tiny bit. "Usually, it means they're lying," he added, lowering it again and lining up his shot.

"Where are you going to go, Henry? This was your getaway plan, wasn't it? You came to live in Creuse, fixed up a dirt cheap house using the cash you got from selling the stolen jewels to pay traders - who would be grateful for the tax break, rather than suspicious - and disappeared from society without anyone knowing where you'd gone... but you thought Fern was onto you, didn't you?" I asked, playing for time and hoping that Jaques would listen to his phone messages soon. I also hoped that the email Marius had sent hadn't been offensive enough for him to write the whole thing off as a strange joke. If we got out of here alive, I would be having words with Marius about past decisions potentially causing future problems.

Henry's lips twitched up like I'd just said something funny. His impossibly dark hair shone in the warm light of the room, and his designer shoes shifted. "Stupid criminals always flee to the Costa Del Sol. Smart ones pick somewhere that's not swarming with police - who carry photos of you in their wallets and can book return tickets to dear old England, faster than a student on a gap year who's run out of money."

"You're definitely not a dumb criminal. Your first crime may not have gone entirely to plan, when you accidentally appeared on videotape after your jewel stealing contraption failed, but you still got away with it. You got away with it for decades... by coming to Creuse. You probably imagined that it was water under the bridge... until you discovered that a popular true crime podcast was digging up your cold case. Did you have an alert set up for certain keywords?" I asked, wanting to know if I was right about this part.

Henry shrugged, before glancing down at his gun and back up again - making the very visual decision that it didn't matter what he told us now, because this was the end of the road for one of us... and he didn't expect it to be him. "Yeah, sure. Anyone who can turn on a computer can set up an alert. I got pinged as soon as that podcast put out the episode. I thought the name sounded familiar, but I didn't know why until Miranda mentioned that Fern had asked for a dentist recommendation and Ursula had given her the name of the man we all use. I suddenly remembered that at one of Damien's get-togethers the previous year, Fern had come with us to the group and got chatty with Lyra about true crime. They were both really excited to have met another fan." Here, Henry rolled his eyes - the criminal apparently not impressed by wannabe sleuths and historians. "I heard Fern going on about a podcast, where old crime cases were discussed and sometimes even solved by the podcasters and the listeners working together. I didn't remember the name of it until it popped up on the alert, and I suddenly remembered that it was the same one she'd mentioned back then." He sucked in a breath. "With that and the dentist thing seeming like too much of a coincidence… I took a look at the podcast."

"And you saw the CCTV. The footage would have been available back when you committed the crime, but this time around, something was different. Technology has moved on since it was filmed, and a pioneering new technique that the podcast is famous for using had enhanced it, making it crisp enough for certain details to become more visible… like the scar on your face," I cut in and watched as Henry's left cheek twitched unconsciously.

Now was not the time for smiling, but I felt a sense of satisfaction knowing that I was right. "The scar in the video bothered me, because I knew I hadn't seen it on anyone, which made me wonder if the podcast was even relevant. I did initially wonder if Fern had been using her knowledge of the dentist's extra services against certain others, who might have regretted what they'd shared with Fern and decided to silence her, if she'd threatened to spill the details."

Henry frowned. "Extra services? Doctor Schmeical just does dental work. My gold tooth was too distinctive, so I paid him to replace it with a white veneer," he said, apparently oblivious to what I still strongly suspected his wife was getting up to with the dentist. "When Miranda told me that Fern was asking around for recommendations, I knew that she was trying to find out about my tooth. That stupid video... if it weren't for the scar..."

"What scar?!" Marius loudly whispered to me.

"The one he's hiding with those stick on sideburns," I said. "It was actually Marius who made me realise what you'd done, even though I'd seen the evidence at the wake without realising it. He used the phrase 'scarred for life', reminding me that scars do indeed last for a lifetime... and hair certainly doesn't grow back over them. It's something that Fern would have been very conscious of - having scars of her own that she did her best to conceal by never tying up her hair. It's also probably the reason why she noticed your scar and remembered it far more clearly than anyone else might have done. The hair dye is obvious, but not suspicious - given that many men of your age would like to recapture some of their youth and don't always pick the most believable colours to do it. The sideburns - although faintly ridiculous and noticed by the others at Damien's birthday party for being new - are convincing, and perfect for covering up a scar at a time when others might start looking for it. I only spotted something was amiss at the wake when what looked like a droplet of sweat remained by one of your sideburns after you'd wiped your face. That was how I realised it was something else... glue. You must have spilled some when reapplying the sideburns, and it stayed on your face - shinier than skin and a dead giveaway that something fishy was going on."

"Cheers for explaining all of that. It's good to know that after all these years, there's still no decent proof that I actually did anything," Henry said with a smirk.

"Oh, but there *is* proof," I countered, tilting my head at the obnoxious man in front of me. "You're wearing it right now."

Henry made no move, but I sensed he was suddenly alert.

"The star of the exhibition at *Precious Pebbles* was a black diamond with crimson depths. Selling something that distinctive would have been hard, and keeping it as a trophy would also have been a move that could get you caught one day. But you couldn't resist keeping it, could you? Or rather… a piece of it. Your stud earring flashes red when the light hits it," I finished, having observed the colour the very first time I'd met Henry. "The only thing I don't understand is why Ursula is wearing a ring that features fragments of the same stolen diamond. Fern asked her about it, so she must have noticed the same thing that I did… but Ursula implied that she and I weren't the only ones who'd asked her questions about the ring."

"You'd better believe she wasn't the first one to spot that ring!" Henry exploded, making me think this was something that had bothered him for a long time. "The other jewellery was easy enough to shift for cash with the contacts I've built up, but the black one…" He shook his head. "I had it cut into smaller stones, so it could be sold without anyone tracing it back too easily. It didn't make me as much money as it should have done, but that's the risk you take with something so high profile. I kept a small stone as a souvenir, but what I wasn't expecting was for the local jeweller I'd paid double to stay silent about all of this to try his luck, by flogging a ring he'd made with some of the chips via a pawnshop. I guess he thought I wouldn't notice it that way, but Ursula the jewellery expert happened upon it. I'm sure she knew there was something dodgy about the ring when it must have been sold for a bargain price, but she must have liked it enough that she never wanted to investigate further. She probably just thought she'd bought stolen jewellery. A lot of that ends up in pawnshops."

"Instead, she was buying a small piece of a stolen diamond," I observed, wondering how many things could have been different if Ursula had decided to investigate what she had bought.

Henry moved his lips back and forth, like talking about the sideburns had caused them to itch. "You know, I'm glad we had this conversation. I did wonder if I'd overreacted to Fern getting in touch with the dentist, even though I knew she would have seen the footage and might have recognised my scar - being the busy body that she was. That alone is not proof of anything at all, but if she was close enough to be asking Ursula about her ring, then I was right all along."

"So you decided to cut her investigation short," I said, unable to hide the distaste in my voice. "You were a thief, Henry, not a murderer. Why would you take such an extreme step, instead of just running away?"

I didn't like the way that Henry smiled at my words. "What makes you think that the jewellery heist was my first time stepping over the line that society demands we remain behind? The jewellery thing made the headlines because of money, but some crimes… some crimes stay quiet from start to finish."

A chill crawled up my spine when I realised that I hadn't solved the entire mystery of Henry Jones after all. The man I was talking to was someone who completely lacked empathy for others and hid it beneath a veneer of charisma. Any obstacle that stood in his way was an obstacle he would be willing to remove without a second thought. Fern had been one such obstacle to him, and now we had become another… destined to be done away with, before Henry would likely finally decide to run, now that he knew people were definitely looking more closely at his past.

"How did you get so good at making things, Henry?" I asked, curious about how this man had got to be where he was today.

"Degrees are overrated. I worked as an apprentice at a factory where the machines were always breaking. That kind of thing gives you real skills... more than those university educated toffs have got. I can fix just about anything, and solve just about any problem," he added more chillingly.

"Like Damien's car," I suddenly remembered.

"Yep. It was a piece of cake. All of the odd jobs I do around here are easy for me. Obviously, I don't actually need the money, but I'm a smart guy... I know you can't be sitting around, looking like you don't need to work to get by. People start asking questions. I just picked a job that I was good at anyway and treated it like a hobby."

"Too bad you couldn't have stuck with doing your 'hobby' to make an honest living," I commented.

"Well, it looks like you put together the whole picture. Congratulations," Henry said, pretending to applaud, by tapping one hand against the butt of the rifle for a moment. "You've also made it even more abundantly clear how important it is that I kill you and get out of here, before anyone else plays detective and puts the pieces together." He glanced out of the window and his forehead creased with annoyance for a second, before he returned his attention to the task at hand - killing us.

"You don't like loose ends, do you?" I blurted, thinking on my feet. Anything to buy us a few more seconds, while we either figured out some miraculous plan of escape that hadn't occurred to me thus far (unlikely) or the gendarmes finally did their jobs well enough to be useful (maybe even less likely). All in all, beyond a few final bluffs, things weren't looking too good for me and Marius - who was undoubtedly wishing that aggressive geese were the biggest of his problems right now.

"That is stating the obvious, but thank you for reminding me that I have a job to do," he said, shaking his head and moving his finger towards the trigger.

"Lyra… you're probably wondering where she is, aren't you?" I spat out, my brain saying anything it could to extend its survival beyond the next few seconds.

Henry sighed and removed his finger again. "As you've already pointed out, I am not your average dumb criminal, and I'm also well aware that you will probably say just about anything you think I want to hear, in order to stop me from pulling this trigger. I don't think you know where Lyra is. If you did, you wouldn't have wandered in here looking for her and had the bad luck of meeting me, when I'd hidden my car and was also waiting for her to return from the gendarmes. It always pays to be sure you've finished the job," he added - apparently a thief and a murderer with a penchant for quality control. "I know all of that talk about a mysterious letter from Fern was probably nonsense. The perfunctory traps she'd set up around this place before I got here showed me that she was hoping to catch Fern's killer red-handed, because she had no evidence, and maybe even no clue as to who she was hoping to catch. But you can't trap the master of traps." He allowed himself a chortle. "It's a shame really. I could have given her a few tips. I even left the tripwire across the gate intact. That one being sprung would have been a dead giveaway that I was here… and that there might be some surprises waiting for her inside the house." He tapped his temple with a finger for a moment, keeping his finger on the trigger. "Clever, see? This gun is hers, too. She hadn't rigged it into a trap, but I'm sure I can make it look like she did… and then it went off, tragically killing two innocent bystanders who were here to check on her safety. Or snooping around where their noses didn't belong... whichever shoe fits best." He shrugged to show that he didn't care which way it would be spun, so long as we both ended up dead. "I might not even have to leave town. Everything will be put on Lyra the mechanical engineer, who has so conveniently demonstrated how good she is at making deadly traps... and life will continue as normal. I don't know what you told your gendarme friend, or if you actually told him anything at all, but I bet he'll go for that story. Especially when there's no proof of anything else," he added, tapping his earring in a way that made me think it wouldn't be staying in his ear for long after this conversation.

"You're right... about everything," I said, shrugging my shoulders in resignation. "We did come in here looking for Lyra because we had no idea where she was and thought we might be too late to save her, but I do know where she is right now," I added with a victorious smile.

Henry's eyes clouded with concern for a moment, before he did exactly what I'd been hoping and turned to look behind him. It was an old trick, and one that was easy to see through if you stopped to think about everything Henry had pointed out about me being willing to say just about anything to get him to refrain from filling us both with lead - but I'd been relying on that split second of doubt forcing his head to turn, before his logical mind had a chance to catch up.

Unfortunately, all of the psychological tricks in the world don't make up for a distinct lack of athletic ability, so when I threw myself towards Henry's legs, hoping that my second rugby tackle of the evening would be just as effective as the last one, I realised that I was not going to get anywhere close with my hopeful leap.

I landed on the wooden floorboards in front of Henry with a painful thump that whipped his head back around. It succeeded in drawing his attention for the extra split second Marius had needed to get close enough to Henry with the umbrella he'd seized from the stand by the front door. Henry realised his mistake and brought the gun up again at the same moment that Marius clobbered him in the face with the old-fashioned brolly. There was a blast that made my ears ring and my brain seem to shake, as I pushed myself up off the floor and rushed to see what had happened.

Henry had dropped the gun, the shot happily going straight into the ceiling. Now, he and Marius were wrestling on the floor. Marius was smaller than the bulky criminal, but he was holding his own and had the advantage of the umbrella, which he was using to whack Henry into submission at regular intervals.

"Give up! Surrender!" Marius shouted over and over again in French, as well as adding in a few other words that it was probably best not to repeat.

It was the sound of a car crunching on the gravel outside that finally ended the fight. With a roar like a wounded hippo, Henry managed to throw Marius off through sheer desperation and stood up again. His eyes searched the room for the gun, but I'd already kicked it underneath a rather fancy bureau, knowing that it was better away from the fight than in the hands of someone who didn't know how to use it (me). Muttering curses, the murderer turned around and fled back through the house he'd entered to kill those who'd learned the truth about a past he'd been running from for years. And now, he was running again.

But this time, he didn't get far.

"Henry Jones, you are under arrest for the murder of Fern Higgle and for… anything else you might have done inside her house," Jaques Laurent said from where he'd caught the fleeing man just beyond the backdoor. "Are you alive in there?!" he yelled a moment later.

I exchanged a look with Marius, both of us unimpressed that Jaques had arrived at the right moment to take all of the credit for catching the criminal, but not in a timely enough manner to have helped us in any way, shape, or form when we'd been fighting for our lives.

"Yes!" I shouted back reluctantly.

"No thanks to you!" Marius added.

For once, I didn't correct him.

"Glad to hear it. You can make your own way back, can't you?" Jaques said, apparently well and truly done with us both, now that he had his man.

"Shouldn't you be taking our statements?" I called back, wondering why we were shouting at each other, before deciding it was probably better this way. I would be sorely tempted to borrow Marius' umbrella and do some clobbering of my own if Jaques were standing in front of me.

"Someone will take them from you at some point. I'll send a team in to secure any evidence," he yelled back.

"Do we have to tell them about the traps?" Marius asked me in a quieter voice.

"Yes," I replied, grudgingly. With one last sigh, I followed the path that Henry had taken through the house and out of the open backdoor, making certain that I didn't touch anything or tread anywhere that he hadn't.

"Ah, there you are," Jaques said, having palmed Henry off on one of his subordinates. "All safe and well, I hope?" he added, not exactly convincingly. Part of me suddenly wondered if he'd been hoping that something bad - or even fatal - would have befallen us, because it would make the case that much more clear-cut for the captain of the gendarmes, who was undoubtedly still in the dark about exactly why he'd just arrested the man who'd run from the house.

"When did you get the message I left you?" I asked, more interested in grilling the gendarme than the killer.

"Did you struggle to get through? My phone battery ran out and messages left on the landline don't always get recorded. Luckily, I check my emails pretty regularly," he said with a frown that made me think I definitely needed to check whatever it was that Marius had sent in addition to our plea for backup. "It worked out rather well in the end, didn't it?"

"For you," Marius muttered.

"Where is Lyra?" I asked him, having seen no trace of her inside the house and no sign of her now, either.

"Some place that's not here... which shows she's smarter than we are," Marius said, shaking his head.

"She left the gendarmerie almost immediately after I brought her back there, when she revealed that she had been lying about receiving something from Fern but wouldn't explain why. Our translator said she was trying to pass it off as something silly she'd said after drinking too much. In the end, I had someone take her back to her house."

"Where she then set up traps for the killer, hoping that they would come for her and not suspect that she was ready for them." I looked around at the surrounding fields. "She's either close by, or waiting until morning to come back. I doubt she drank anything at all at the wake," I added, seeing Lyra's entire misguided plan for what it was - a simple ruse with bait she'd hoped the killer of unknown identity would take.

He did his best to look dismissive of what I'd just said, but I saw the realisation that he'd been used dawning in his eyes. "The point is, the case has been solved and everyone is safe. A happy ending for all." He attempted to smile at me and Marius, but gave up when he saw our expressions. "No need to thank me for stopping the killer from getting away," he added flippantly - which with hindsight, he would probably view as a fatal mistake.

"It seems like you have everything under control. We'll leave you to it," I said, deciding that Jaques had been given all the help he would be getting. When he finally realised he lacked concrete evidence - beyond witness statements - and discovered that Henry was a slippery customer, I knew he would come looking for us.

"Don't touch the front door handle," Marius added - surprising me by being so thoughtful.

We turned away from Jaques, taking the long way around the side of the house to return to where Marius had parked the car.

"I only said about the door because otherwise, he might have left everything in place for when Lyra gets back. Can you imagine how incompetent it would be if the next victim was murdered *after* he'd already arrested the killer?"

"Unfortunately, I can imagine it," I said, equally darkly. When Jaques and his colleagues had turned up so promptly after Fern's untimely death, they'd seemed to be interested in investigating what could be nothing other than a brutal, premeditated murder. I'd hoped that Marius' and my sleuthing days were over, and the gendarmes would take something so serious, well… seriously. The conclusion of this case had revealed that the thing Jaques was best at doing was arriving after the action had taken place to wrap things up with a neat bow and pat himself on the back.

"I can't believe he's going to get all of the credit for this," Marius said, thinking along the same lines that I had been.

"It's true, he is going to get the credit… but not until he comes to ask us how we solved his case for him," I said with a small smile of victory when we got back into the car.

Marius considered. "He doesn't know about the earring or the sideburns, does he?"

"When he comes to see us, we'll be only too happy to help him wrap things up for good."

"Will we?" Marius commented, looking unimpressed.

"We will… with certain terms and conditions attached."

The sound of someone clearing his throat made both of us turn around when we were on the cusp of reaching the car. A young gendarme stood just behind us, looking like a sudden movement might cause him to dash off in a panic. "I was wondering if I could talk to you… Monsieur Bisset," he clarified, when Marius and I exchanged a look.

"Fine," Marius said with great reluctance, before turning back to me. "If Jaques thinks that he can send underlings to grovel for answers, he is sorely mistaken."

"Be nice," I gently chided Marius, knowing that the young man was probably caught up in the crossfire and didn't deserve the same treatment as the man in charge of this farce of an investigation - a man… who I was unsurprised to find approaching the car after Marius had been spirited away by the young gendarme. Jaques may be a pretty poor investigator, but he was fairly good at manipulating others to go and do what he wanted.

He smiled when we made eye contact, but I kept my own mouth pressed in a thin line. "Is there something you want to ask me?" I suggested.

"Ah, I… yes," Jaques confessed, his smile turning sheepish. "It's just, I would value your expertise on how events transpired to bring us all to this end point. It would be good to get a second opinion on certain things."

I shot him a withering look. "Things like… the lack of evidence you find yourself facing, along with slim to no knowledge about the motive for all of this?"

"I know certain things," Jaques bristled, but he swiftly calmed down again when he remembered that he needed this conversation to go his way.

"You're right. I do have everything that you need… so long as you take that earring Henry is wearing from him right away and keep it safe and secure. It's the key to you solving the murder, attempted murder, and the jewellery heist which led to all of it. I will tell you how it all fits together, but first, I want us to get a few things straight. There are going to be some changes to the way things are done around here…"

* * *

"I suppose the other gendarme was sent to keep you busy whilst I chatted with Jaques?" I said when Marius finally returned and we slid back inside the car. "Jaques can't bear to do anything without it being an exercise in psychology. He's probably in the wrong job, although I dread to think what the right one would be. I sorted everything out with him. He wasn't too happy about my terms and conditions and threatened me with obstruction of justice charges." I rolled my eyes, knowing that Jaques would never have proceeded with his threats, given that it would lead to a review of his own failings. "In the end, I told him everything we found out. In return for that, Jaques will bring us both on as paid consultants if something like this ever occurs again in the future. We'll essentially do everything we did this time around, but receive compensation and recognition for doing it."

"But he'll still get any future arrests under his belt," Marius countered.

I shrugged and shook my ashy curls. "There's no perfect solution, but it's something at least, isn't it? At the end of the day, I know you and I want to do the right thing for others. It's why we picked our respective careers. Perhaps we'll rub off on Jaques eventually. Or perhaps life will be quieter around here from now on."

"Don't count on it," Marius said with a shake of his head. "The world is changing… even our little corner of it." We both paused to reflect on that for a second. "He wasn't trying to distract me, by the way - the other gendarme. At least, I don't think he was. He sounded very genuine and nervous… like he'd be in trouble if he was caught."

"What did he want? Did he ask you out on a date?" I asked with my tongue pressed firmly into my cheek as we pulled away from the deadly dwelling.

"No, although, I do look very handsome today," Marius said, winking at himself in the rearview mirror and making me laugh. "Actually… he asked me if I would give him a job. He wants to leave the gendarmes… and join the Sellenoise Municipal Police. I've finally found my new recruit."

19

PICK YOUR BATTLES

It was a balmy day in September when Damien threw himself another party.

When the written invitation had arrived looking so much like the first, I had hesitated a good long time before getting back to him. It was only when Marius had dropped in, waving his own invitation in disgust that I'd decided to tell him I was going, just to wind him up. I wasn't normally so petty, but ever since Olivier Lavigne had quit his job working as a gendarme and transferred to Sellenoise's local police force, Marius had become impossible - crowing to anyone who'd listen about how he'd snatched new talent from the jaws of the establishment.

Olivier himself was actually a rather nice young man, which made his desire to exit the gendarme clique understandable. He was younger than Marius with hair the colour of sand, and a silver earring that I'd caught Marius looking sideways at - making me wonder whether he was thinking of saying something hypocritical (given his own tattoos) or considering getting one for himself.

Olivier had experienced life at the bottom of the pile

when he'd worked for the gendarmes. Although he knew he wasn't going to be ruling the roost in Sellenoise, I'd been able to tell that making a difference to people's lives, and having a community he was responsible for, appealed to him. We'd met a couple of times when I'd been doing some more work to sort out the station's terrible filing system. He'd been quiet and respectful - shy at first, but once I'd discovered that he enjoyed sewing for a hobby, we'd bonded over our love of crafting - before he'd made me promise not to share it with Marius, in case the chief of police thought it was silly. I had countered that by telling him that Marius had some unusual hobbies of his own, and I would share what they were if he tried to mock Olivier. When that got back to Marius, I knew he'd be concerned about which hobby I was talking about, and what I might know that he had not knowingly shared - even though I actually knew nothing of the sort. While I'd joked about it with Olivier, I knew that Marius would never seriously heap scorn on someone else in that way. He liked to posture in front of those he thought would take advantage of any perceived weakness, but he was a good man, and a remarkably perceptive and understanding one when he stopped strutting about.

Beneath Olivier's concerns about Marius, I had heard the echo of how his previous job had treated him. I held on to all the hope in my heart that this would be a different, and better start in policing for the young man. One thing it did mean for sure was that I would no longer be chained to the filing cabinets every spare moment I had. With Marius finally having help, as soon as Olivier settled into the new routine, I was certain that I would be spending more time at home, continuing with the house renovations - something that was very much needed, with winter creeping ever closer. I was determined that this year, Spice and I would not spend all of the months between November and March clothed in a minimum of three layers of knitwear.

All of that was actually the other reason I'd decided to say yes to Damien's second written invitation of the summer - I was worried my life might get a little too quiet in the near future, and I wasn't sure how I felt about that. But even though it was true that everyone needed a little excitement in their lives, I was hoping that Damien's party wouldn't be *too* exciting.

"I can't believe you talked me into this," Marius grumbled when we pulled up outside of Damien's grey house with its bright red front door.

"I think it sounds like fun!" Olivier interjected from the backseat. "I didn't expect to be invited to a party so soon after starting work here."

I smiled at him in the rearview mirror, pleased that at least someone was enthusiastic about this. Damien had wasted no time in inviting the new police agent - always keen to include anyone new to the area, in order to extract every juicy detail about them that he could.

"I'm sure it will be enjoyable. Damien always excels at food," I told him, feeling a little bad about resorting to merely congratulating the culinary element, but when I knew what the company was like, it was a case of 'if you can't say anything nice, don't say anything at all'.

Miranda hadn't been there when the gendarmes had gone to talk to her after arresting her husband. They'd found her things gone and her car missing, which rather led me to believe she hadn't been oblivious to her husband's past. Something had pinged in my mind when Jaques had called to ask if I had any information that might help find her. I hadn't been able to assist with that, but I'd suddenly remembered that Miranda's job sometimes required her to help fashion leaders to put on exhibitions. Exhibitions… like the one that had been at *Precious Pebbles* when Henry had robbed it. He'd had insider information after all.

The whole story had got back to the *Cold Case Crackers* podcast, and they had recorded an entire episode in tribute to Fern, who had come so close to solving the case herself. Miranda's image had been shared so widely that I doubted even the quietest of towns in the country would fail to recognise her. If she had committed a crime, or knowingly concealed the crimes of another, she would be brought to justice.

"Don't expect anything criminal to happen," Marius said, still keen to burst Olivier's bubble of enthusiasm. "Life in Sellenoise is normally very quiet. The most exciting thing you'll see all week will be some escaped chickens. It's not all murder and mayhem."

"I know that," Olivier said humbly, as we walked up the path towards Damien's house. He darted ahead and rang the bell for us. To the young man's bemusement, Marius grabbed the back of his collar and hauled him several feet back from the door… which suddenly swung outwards and hit the lavender bushes that grew along the sides of the path.

"Hellooooo!" Damien said, waving a very spiky morning star over his head. "You won't believe what came in the post today. Isn't it beautiful?" He showed off the studded metal ball that swung back and forth on a chain attached to a long handle.

Olivier's face split into a grin, whilst Marius' own expression turned thunderous.

"I thought he just said everything around here was boring?" Olivier said to me in a stage whisper.

"What are you doing with that thing?" Marius growled, furious about Damien unknowingly undermining him. "Haven't you got enough of them already… and done enough harm?!"

Damien blinked. "I have been finding it a bit challenging to find places to hang my newest purchases, which is why some items were stored elsewhere." He rubbed his chin for a moment, apparently dwelling on what had happened in the barn with one such stored weapon. "You may have a point."

"Finally!" Marius said, throwing his hands up in the air and looking pleased and furious all at the same time. Damien had always managed to annoy him to the point of him searching for a reason to arrest the man. So far, Damien hadn't actually done anything provably criminal, but that didn't stop Marius from hoping he'd slip up one day.

"I was thinking I could give some of my less needed items to the *Emmaüs* charity shop I heard is being set up in Sellenoise - a lovely idea, by the way. It's always good to see old things recycled and reused, instead of being thrown away! Although, people around here usually keep using something until it falls to pieces, so I don't know what sort of state they're going to get their items in. Yet another reason why I should contribute."

"An *Emmaüs* shop won't accept weapons," Marius said, doing a remarkable job of keeping his emotions under control - even though I sensed smoke was about to pour from his ears.

"What about decorative pieces or antiques? It's not like I'm going to be handing them a loaded pistol. Those are all staying safely with me," he added with a wink in my direction.

"You keep them loaded?!" Marius spluttered, before he regained his composure, probably hoping he was being toyed with. "No dumping your deadly weapons at any shops, or even giving them away to anyone who fancies taking up fencing. Need I remind you that the last three fatal incidents in Sellenoise can all be traced back to your idiotic acquisitions?!"

"My dear Marius, I thought that, being our beloved chief of police, you would know better than anyone that medieval weapons don't kill people... people kill people! Let's be sensible about all this."

"Sensible?! Sensible!" The protest died in Marius' mouth before he could finish it, realising that he was fighting a losing battle. "No giving weapons away... and no charity shops," he grunted.

"Yes, yes... all right," Damien relented - so cheerfully that I had a sneaking suspicion that this entire conversation had been contrived to show Marius how things could be so much worse, if Damien decided to deliberately distribute his instruments of death among the community. A community, who were already more than capable of doing harm to themselves and others, with the amount of farm machinery and hunting paraphernalia kicking about the place. Apparently in the mood to push his luck, he extended the handle of the morning star towards the chief of police. "Fancy a go?"

"I would love to!" Olivier announced, trying to sidestep Marius, who swiftly shoved him into the lavender. "Wow! You're enthusiastic! I guess I'll take the second turn," Olivier said, struggling to get back up with his hair all over the place.

"Handle it carefully," Damien prattled on. "Accidents do happen!"

"Yes, they do... with alarming regularity," Marius agreed, reaching out for the morning star with far too much careful consideration.

This time, he was the one who ended up in the lavender when I pushed him off the path.

"Time for food?" I suggested.

"Of course! It's always time for food. Come in, come in... the others aren't here yet, but there's no reason at all why we can't get started," he said brightly, placing the morning star down on his hall table when I followed him inside.

"Damien…" I said, glancing down at the terrifyingly designed weapon.

"Yes? Ah, oh… probably shouldn't leave that there, should I?" He sheepishly picked it up again and trotted through into the main hall, where he hung the weapon up on a waiting stand, stopping to admire it for a second. The paper tag with 'Property of Damien Rue' written on it wiggled in the draught caused by the front door being open - where two police agents were presumably still pulling themselves out of the lavender. "Maybe I should invest in more security… you know, to keep these things safe."

"I think that's an excellent idea," I said, wholeheartedly endorsing the plan.

"Yes, I've always wanted to have a go at making my own burglar deterrent. I think it could be rather fun!"

I took a breath to tell him that 'making his own' was absolutely not what I'd had in mind. I knew the sort of thing Damien would think was a good idea, and it probably wouldn't be too far off something Henry Jones would approve of. "I think things are probably fine the way they are," I allowed, knowing I'd fallen for the same trick as Marius.

"Jolly good," Damien called back from the kitchen. "I thought they might be," he added, confirming my earlier impression that the older man knew exactly how to present a worst case scenario in order to make what he was currently doing look like the sensible, safe option.

"Damien…" I called, wondering whether to point out that I knew exactly what he was doing, and that he couldn't bury his head in the sand forever.

"Yes?" he enquired, returning carrying a tray of drinks and a plate of homemade nibbles.

I considered the food being placed in front of me. "You haven't forgotten how to throw a good party," I told him, knowing that some things could be changed, eroded over time and perhaps made into something new and improved, while others were constant and life parted around them, like a rock in a river. The rock could not be moved, but the river could bend. "Just... maybe curate your guest lists a little more carefully in the future."

"Absolutely! No more killers for coffee, or murderers for mid-afternoon tea," he agreed enthusiastically - showing that some bending may indeed be possible.

"Great! That's music to my ears," I said, knowing that you couldn't win a stunning victory in every single battle you decided to fight.

Especially when the person you were fighting against owned enough weapons to arm a small country.

BOOKS IN THE SERIES

The French Fraud
The French Folly
The French Fiasco
The French Fancy

A REVIEW IS WORTH ITS WEIGHT IN GOLD!

I really hope you enjoyed reading this story. I was wondering if you could spare a couple of moments to rate and review this book? As an indie author, one of the best ways you can help support my dream of being an author is to leave me a review on your favourite online book store, or even tell your friends.

Reviews help other readers, just like you, to take a chance on a new writer!

Thank you!
Myrtle Morse

ALSO BY MYRTLE MORSE

COURTSIDE CAFE MYSTERIES

Murder at Match Point

A Volley of Lies

Tennis Balls and a Body

Drop Shots and Disaster

Aces and Accidents

BOOKS BY MYRTLE MORSE WRITING AS RUBY LOREN:

THE WITCHES OF WORMWOOD MYSTERIES

Mandrake and a Murder

Vervain and a Victim

Feverfew and False Friends

Aconite and Accusations

Belladonna and a Body

Prequel: Hemlock and Hedge

MADIGAN AMOS ZOO MYSTERIES

Penguins and Mortal Peril

The Silence of the Snakes

Murder is a Monkey's Game

Lions and the Living Dead

The Peacock's Poison

A Memory for Murder

Whales and a Watery Grave
Chameleons and a Corpse
Foxes and Fatal Attraction
Monday's Murderer
Prequel: Parrots and Payback

DIANA FLOWERS FLORICULTURE MYSTERIES

Gardenias and a Grave Mistake
Delphiniums and Deception
Poinsettias and the Perfect Crime
Peonies and Poison
The Lord Beneath the Lupins

Prequel: The Florist and the Funeral

HOLLY WINTER MYSTERIES

Snowed in with Death
A Fatal Frost
Murder Beneath the Mistletoe
Winter's Last Victim

EMILY MANSION OLD HOUSE MYSTERIES

The Lavender of Larch Hall
The Leaves of Llewellyn Keep
The Snow of Severly Castle
The Frost of Friston Manor
The Heart of Heathley House

JANUARY CHEVALIER SUPERNATURAL MYSTERIES

Death's Dark Horse

Death's Hexed Hobnobs
Death's Endless Enchanter
Death's Ethereal Enemy
Death's Last Laugh
Prequel: Death's Reckless Reaper

Printed in Great Britain
by Amazon